Strauss, Richard

Salome Musik-Drama in einem Aufzuge

Strauss, Richard

Salome Musik-Drama in einem Aufzuge

Inktank publishing, 2018

www.inktank-publishing.com

ISBN/EAN: 9783750128149

Meinem Freunde Sir EDGAR SPEYER.

SALOME.

Musik-Drama in einem Aufzuge
nach OSCAR WILDE'S gleichnamiger Dichtung
In deutscher Übersetzung von Hedwig Lachmann.

Musik
von

RICHARD STRAUSS.

Op. 54.

Klavier-Auszug mit Text
von
OTTO SINGER.

Preis M. 16.— netto.
Prix Fr. 20.— net.

BERLIN – PARIS.
ADOLPH FÜRSTNER.

A. 5503 F.

Personen:

Herodes	Tenor
Herodias	Mezzosopran
Salome	Sopran
Jochanaan	Bariton
Narraboth	Tenor
Ein Page der Herodias	Alt
5 Juden	4 Tenöre, 1 Bass
2 Nazarener	Tenor, Bass
2 Soldaten, Ein Cappadocier	Bässe
Ein Sklave	

Schauplatz der Handlung:
Eine grosse Terrasse im Palast des Herodes.

The Persons of the Music-Drama:

Herod Antipas, Tetrarch of Judæa	Tenor
Herodias, Wife of the Tetrarch	Mezzosoprano
Salome, Daughter of Herodias	Soprano
Jokanaan, The Prophet	Baritone
Narraboth, The young Syrian	Tenor
The Page of Herodias	Contralto
5 Jews	4 Tenors, 1 Bass
2 Nazarenes	Tenor, Bass
2 Soldiers, A Cappadocian	Basses
A Slave	

Synopsis of Scenery:
A great terrace in the Palace of Herod.

A. 5508. 5540 F.

SALOME

von | by

Richard Strauss.

 A 5503 F Berlin, Adolph Fürstner.

Nar.
selt - sam. Wie ei - ne klei - ne Prin - zes - sin, de-ren
strange look. She is like a prin - cess who has
sempre dolcissimo
Füs - se weisse Tau - ben sind. Man könnte mei-nen, sie
litt - le snow-white doves as feet. You would fancy she was
pp
mf
Page.
3
Wie ei - ne Frau, die tot ist.
She's like a pale dead wo - man.
tanzt.
dancing.
pp
Più mosso
4 Etwas lebhafter.
P.
Sie glei-tet langsam da - hin.
She moveth slow-ly a - long.
(Noise in the banqueting hall.)
(Lärm im Bankettsaal.)
First soldier
Erster Soldat.
Was für ein Aufruhr!
What an up-roar!
Etwas lebhafter.
p
f

A. 5503 F

I. S.
Was sind das für wil-de Tie - re, die da
Who are those that like wild a - ni - mals are
heu - len?
howl - ing?
5
ff
Second soldier.
Zweiter Soldat.
Die
They're
Ju - den.
Jews there.
(dryly)
(trocken)
Sie sind immer so.
They are always so.
Sie streiten
They quarrel
First soldier.
Erster Soldat.
6
poco ritard.
Etwas zurückhaltend.
Ich fin-de es lä-cher-lich, ü-ber
I think 'tis ri - di - cu - lous to dis -
ü-ber ih-re Re-li-gion.
a-bout their re - li - gion.
Etwas zurückhaltend.
dim.
pp
mf

Narraboth (warmly) (warm)
Erstes Zeitmass.
Wie schön ist die Prin-zes - sin
How fair is the Prin - cess
sol-che Din-ge zu strei - ten.
pute a - bout all such mat - ter.
Erstes Zeitmass.
pp
p espr.
pp
Page (anxiously) (unruhig)
Du siehst sie im-mer an.
You al-ways look at her.
Sa - lo - me heu - te A - bend!
Sa - lo - mè this ev'-ning!
7
sf p
l.H.
pp
Du siehst sie zu viel an. Es ist ge-fähr - lich,
You look at her too much. It's dan-ge - rous to
sf
p
l.H.
pp
Men-schen auf die - se Art an - zu-sehn.
look at peo-ple in such fash - ion.
8
Schreck - li-ches kann ge -
Ter - rib-le things may
cresc.
mf sf

schehn.
hap-pen.
Narraboth.
Sie ist sehr schön
She is ve - ry fair
heu - te
on this
pp
f
poco f
A-bend.
ev-ning.
First soldier.
Erster Soldat.
Der Te - trarch sieht fin-ster drein.
The Tetrarch's look is dark.
Second soldier.
Zweiter Soldat.
Ja, er sieht finster drein.
Yes, how dark is his look!
p
9
Wie
How
Auf wen blickt er?
At whom is he looking?
Ich weiss nicht.
I know not.
dim.
pp
p

Narr.
blass die Prin - zes-sin ist.
pale is the Prin - cess!
pp
Niemals ha-be ich sie so
Never have I known her to
blass ge - sehn.
look so pale.
sf
p
10
Sie
She
sf
p
ist wie der Schat - ten
is like the sha - dow
ei-ner weis - sen Ro - se
of a snow - white rose
dim.
pp
Page (very anxiously) (sehr unruhig)
Du musst sie nicht an - sehn.
You must not look at her.
Du siehst sie zu
You look at her
in ei-nem sil-ber-nen Spie - gel.
in a mir-ror of sil - ver.
accelerando
cresc.
p
cresc.

Subito molto più lento
M. 𝅗𝅥 = 48
Plötzlich viel ruhiger im Zeitmass.
11
viel an. Schreck - li-ches kann ge - - schehn.
too much. Ter - rible things may hap - pen.
Stimme des Jochanaan (aus der Cisterne)
The voice of Jokanaan (from the cistern)
Nach mir wird
After me shall
M. 𝅗𝅥 = 48
Plötzlich viel ruhiger im Zeitmass.
fz
dim.
ppp
Joch.
Jok.
Ei - ner kom - men, der ist stär - ker als ich.
come an - o - ther who is great - er than I.
12
ppp
sfz
pp
espr.
Ich bin nicht wert, ihm zu lö - sen den Rie - men an sei - nen Schuhn.
I am not worthy so much as to un - loose the latchet of his shoes.
l.H.
13
Wenn er kommt, wer - den die ver - ö - de - ten Stüt - ten froh -
When he comes shall all the de - sert - ed pla - ces be
pp
f pp
dim.
A. 5503 F.

12
Joch. Jok.
lo - cken. Wenn er kommt, wer - den die Au-gen der Blin-den
hap - py. When he comes, shall the eyes of the blind see
ppp
mf pp
f
14
den Tag sehn. Wenn er kommt, die Oh - ren der Tau -
the day - light. When he comes, the ears of the deaf
mf pp
pp
- ben ge - öff - - net.
shall be o - - pened.
poco più mosso
Etwas lebhafter.
Second soldier.
Zweiter Soldat.
Heiss ihn schwei-gen!
Make him be si - lent!
Etwas lebhafter.
f marc.
f
dim.
First soldier.
Erster Soldat.
15
Er ist ein heil'-ger Mann.
He is a ho - ly man.
H.S.
Er sagt im-mer lä-cher-li-che
They are sil - ly things which he is
p
espr.
f
f
dim.
A. 5503 F.

I. S.
II. S.
Er ist sehr sanft. Je-den Tag, den ich ihm zu es-
But he is good. Every day when I bring him food.
Din-ge.
say-ing.
espr.
A Cappadocian.
Ein Cappadocier.
16
Wer ist es?
Who is he?
-sen ge-be, dankt er mir. Ein Pro-
-he gi-veth thanks to me. He's a
p espr.
pp
sfz
Cap.
Wie ist sein Na-me? Wo-her kommt er?
What is his name? Whence comes he?
phet. Jo-cha-na-an. Aus der
prophet. Jo-ka-nu-an. From the
p
espr.
17
Wü-ste. Ei-ne Schaar von Jün- - gern war dort im-mer um
de-sert. A great mul-ti-tude used to fol-low af-ter
A 5503 F

18

Cap. Wo-von re-det er?
Of what does he talk?

1.S. ihn. Un - mög-lich ist's, zu ver - stehn, was er
him. Not one of us un-der - stands what he

sfz *pp* *pp*

Cap. Kann man ihn sehn?
May he be seen?

1.S. sagt. Nein, der Tetrarch hat es ver -
says. No, 'Tis for-bid - den by the

p *cresc.* *f* *p*

19 **Narraboth.** *Noch lebhafter.*

(sehr erregt) Die Prin - zes - sin er - hebt sich! Sie ver-lässt die
(highly excited) Now the Prin-cess is ris - ing! She is leav - ing the

1.S. bo - ten.
Tetrarch.

Più mosso

Noch lebhafter.

f *ff*

Nar. Ta - fel. Sie ist sehr er - regt. Sie
ta - ble! She looks ve - ry trou - bled. She

ff

Page.
20
Sich sie nicht an!
Don't look at her!
Nar.
kommt hierher.
comes this way.
Ja, sie kommt auf uns
Yes, she comes to - wards
ff
dim.
p
L.H.
accelerando
P.
Ich bitte dich, sieh sie nicht an!
I pray you, look not at her!
Nar.
zu.
us.
accelerando
Sie ist
She is
wie eine verirr - te
just like a dove that has
cresc.
Second scene.
Zweite Scene.
(beat full bars)
Presto. Äusserst schnell. (nur ganze Takte schlagen!)
M. 𝅗𝅥.=76
(Salome tritt erregt ein) (Salome enters excited)
Nar.
Tau - - - - be.
stray - - - - ed.
f
p
cresc.
21
Salome
(in changing time)
(in wechselnder Taktart)
Ich will nicht blei - ben. Ich kann nicht blei - ben.
I will not stay. I can - not stay.
f
f

Sal.
22
Wa - rum sieht mich der Tet - rarch fort - während so an
Why, why does the Te-trarch watch me all the while
dim.
pp
23
mit seinen Maul - wurfs - au - gen un - ter den zu - ckenden Li - dern? Es ist
with his mole's eyes from un - der his sha - king eye - lids? It is
p
selt - - - sam, dass der Mann mei - ner Mut - ter mich so an - sieht.
cu - - - rious that the husband of my mo - ther looks at me like
pp
tranquillo
24 ruhiger
that.
p
25
Wie süss ist hier die Luft. Hier kann ich at -
How sweet the air is here. Here I can breathe
p
espr.
A. 5503 F.

26
Sal.
- - - men... Da drin - nen sit - zen Ju - den
With - in are sit - ting Jews
p
mf
aus Je - ru - salem, die ein - an - der ü - ber ih - re när - rischen Ge -
from Je - ru - salem, who are tearing each other to pieces o - ver all their
f
poco a poco più mosso
allmählich lebhafter
bräu - che in Stük - ke rei - ssen.
foo - lish old ce - re - mo - nies.
sfz
ff
dim.
27
Schweig - sa - me, list - ge E - gyp - ter und bru - ta - le, un - ge -
Si - lent and subtle E - gyp - tians, and those bru - tal and bar -
p
pp
mf derb
Ped.
schlachte Rö - mer mit ih - rer plum - pen Spra - che.
ba - rian Ro - mans with their un - couth jar - gon.
cresc.
A. 5503 F

28
Schnell
Presto
Sal.
O, wie ich die-se Rö - mer has-se!
Ah, how I find these Ro - mans hate-ful!
Page.
Schreck-liches wird ge-schehn. Warum
Ter - ri-ble things will happen! Why do you
29 poco calando
überleiten
più tranquillo
wieder ruhiger
Wie
How
Pg.
siehst du sie so an?
look at her so strange?
dim.
gut ist's, in den Mond zu sehn.
good 'tis to see the moon!
Er
She
ist wie ei-ne sil-ber-ne Blu-me,
is like a little sil-ver flow-er,
kühl und
cold and
A. 5508 F.

poco accelerando
30 p
Sal.
keusch. Ja, wie die Schön - heit ei-ner Jungfrau, die rein ge-blie-ben
chaste. I am quite sure she is a virgin, she has a virgin's
poco accelerando (senza cresc.)
espr.
molto più lento che 𝅗𝅥. del 3/4
bedeutend langsamer als 𝅗𝅥. des 3/4 Taktes
ist. Voice of Jokanaan.
beauty
Stimme des Jochanaan.
Sie - he, der Herr ist ge-kom-men, des Menschen Sohn ist
Hear! 'tis the Lord who ap-proacheth, the Son of Man hath
mfpp
pp
Presto
poco più allegro che 𝅗𝅥 del 4/4
31 Sehr schnell. (𝅗𝅥. etwas schneller als 𝅗𝅥 des 4/4)
Wer war das, der hier ge - ru-fen hat?
Who was that, who cry - ed out?
Joch. Jok.
na - he.
come
ff
dim.
32
Zweiter Soldat.
Ach, der Pro - phet.
Ah, 'twas the prophet!
Der Pro - phet, Prin-zes-sin.
'Twas the pro-phet, Princess.
dim.
A 5503 F

20
33
Sal.
Der, vor dem der Tet-rarch Angst hat.
He whom the Tetrarch is a - fraid of.
2.S.
Wir wis-sen da-von nichts, Prin-zes-sin.
We do not know of that, my Princess.
Es war der Pro-phet Jo-cha-na-an, der hier rief.
It was the prophet Jo-ka-na-an who cried out.
34
p
f
dim.
Narraboth (zu Salome) (to Salome)
Be-liebt es Euch, dass ich eu-re Sänf-te ho-len las-se. Prinzessin?
Is it your plea-sure that I bid them bring your lit-ter, my Princess?
pp espr.
Salome
Er sagt schreckli-che Din-ge ü-ber meine
He says terri-ble things, aye, a-bout my
Nar.
Die Nacht ist schön im Gar-ten.
The night is fair in the gar-den.
sf
mf
A 5503 F.

35
Sal.
Mut - ter,
mo - ther,
nicht wahr?
does he not?
Second soldier.
Zweiter Soldat
Wir ver - ste - hen nie, was er
We don't un - der - stand, what he
dim.
pp
Sal.
Ja, er sagt schreckli - che Din - ge ü - ber sie.
Yes, he says ter - ri - ble things a - bout her.
Ein Sklave (eintretend)
A Slave (entering)
Prinzessin,
My Princess,
2 S.
sagt, Prin - zes - sin.
says, my Princess.
mf
cresc.
f
36
(passionately)
(heftig)
Sal.
Ich
I
Skl
der Tetrarch er - sucht Euch, wie - der zum Fest hin - ein zu gehn.
the Te - trarch prays you to re - turn a - gain to the feast.
mf
l.H.
sf

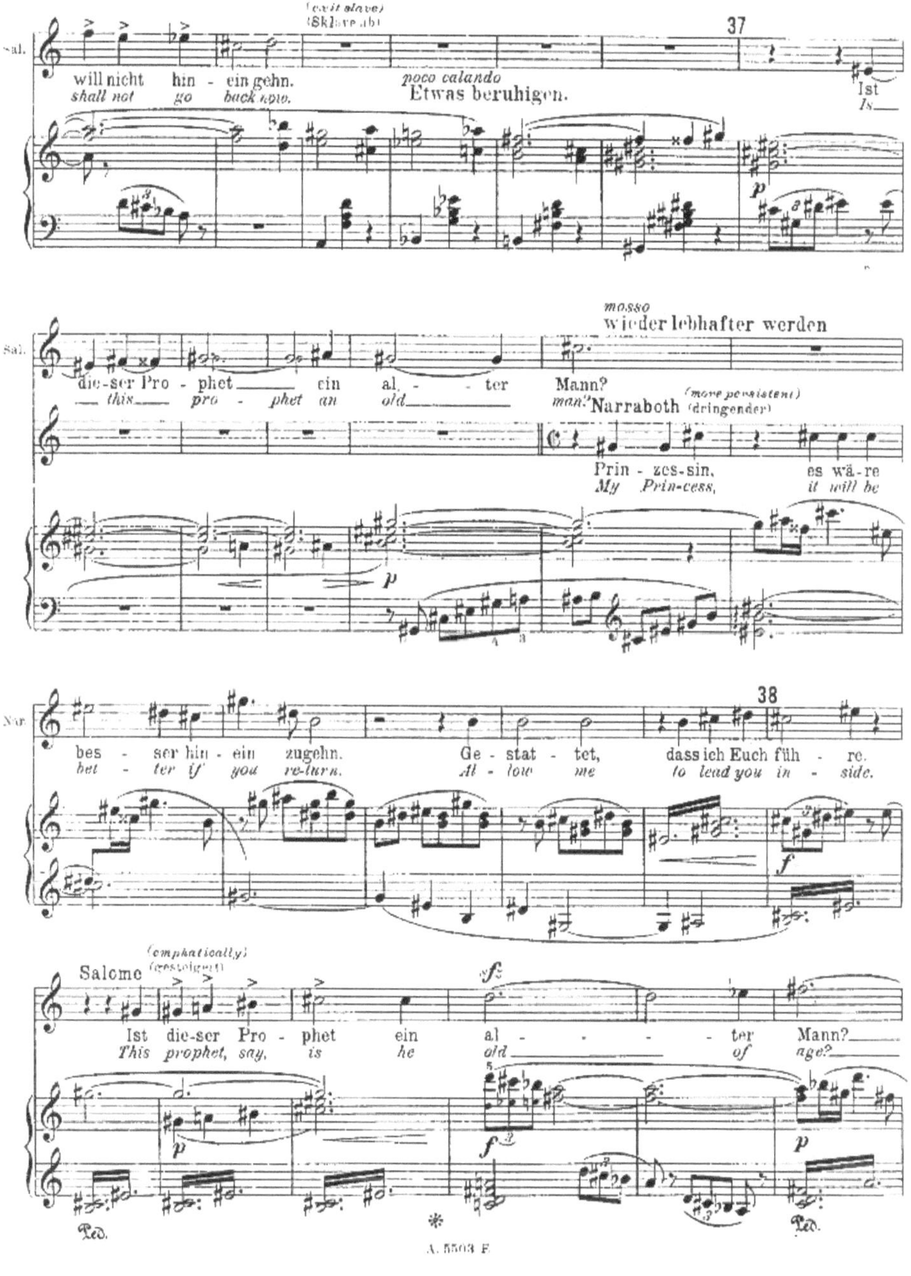

Sal. will nicht hin - ein gehn.
shall not go back now.

(exit slave) (Sklave ab)

poco calando
Etwas beruhigen.

37

Ist dieser Pro - phet ein al - - ter Mann?
Is — this — pro - phet an old — man?

mosso
wieder lebhafter werden

Narraboth (more persistent) (dringender)

Prin - zes-sin, es wä-re bes - ser hin - ein zugehn.
My Prin-cess, it will be bet - ter if you re-turn.

Ge - stat - tet, dass ich Euch füh - re.
Al - low me to lead you in - side.

38

Salome (emphatically) (gesteigert)

Ist die-ser Pro - phet ein al - - - ter Mann?
This prophet, say, is he old — of age?

Ped. * Ped.

Voice of Jokanaan. 23
Sal.
Erster Soldat. First soldier.
Re-
Nein. Prin - zes - sin, er ist ganz
No, my Prin - cess, he is quite
Stimme des Jochanaan
39
Jok.
Jauch-ze nicht, du Land Pa-lä - sti - na weil der Stab des-sen, der dich
joice not thou, land of Pa-les - tine, that the rod of him who did
1 S
jung.
young.
bedeutend langsamer als des 3/4 Taktes
molto più lento che del 3/4
fpp
pp
Joch.
Jok.
schlug, ge - bro - chen ist.
smite thee is bro - ken now.
40 Alla breve.
pp
fp cresc.
sf
p
Denn aus dem Sa - men der Schlan-ge wird ein Ba - si - lisk
For from the seed of the ser - pent, hear, a ba - si - lisk
fpp
fp
A. 5363 F.

24
41
accel.
kom - men und sei - ne Brut wird die
shall come and that which is born of it shall de-
cresc.
f
cresc.
Presto
Sehr schnell. 𝅗𝅥=𝅗𝅥. des 3/4
Salome
Welch selt-sa-me Stimme! Ich möchte mit ihm
How strange does his voice sound! I wish to speak with
Vö - gel ver - schlin - gen.
vour all the birds.
dim.
pp
42
spre - chen.
him now.
Zweiter Soldat. Second soldier.
Prin-zes-sin, der Tetrarch dul-det nicht, dass ir-gend wer mit ihm spricht.
Oh Princess, the Tetrarch does not wish that a-ny one speaks with him.
espr.
cresc.
mf
43
Ich
But
Er hat selbst dem Ho-hen-prie-ster ver - bo - ten, mit ihm zu sprechen.
And e'en the high - priest is for - bid - den to speak with him.
espress.
p

(still more passionate)
(immer heftiger)
44
Sal.
wün - sche mit ihm zu sprechen.
I wish to speak to him now.
Ich
I
2.S.
Es ist un - möglich, Prin - zes - sin.
It is im - possi - ble, Prin - cess.
will mit ihm spre - chen....
wish to speak to him.
accelerando
Bringt diesen Pro - phe - ten her-
Have this prophet brought
45
aus!
forth!
Zweiter Soldat. Second soldier.
Wir dür - fen nicht, Prin - zes - sin.
We dare not, my Prin - cess.
(tritt an die Cisterne heran und blickt hinunter)
(approaching the cistern and looking down)
Lento.
Langsam. M. 𝅗𝅥=60
Wie schwarz es da drun-ten ist!
How black it is down be-low!
espr.
dim.
A. 5593 F.

Sal.

Es muss schrecklich sein in so ei-ner schwarzen Höh - le zu le - ben...
Oh how ter - ri - ble, how ter - ri - ble to be in so black a pit...

ppp *poco marcato*

46

Es ist wie ei - ne Gruft....
It is much like a tomb...

fp *dim.* *ppp*

(wildly)
(wild)

Habt ihr nicht ge - hört?
Well, did you not hear me?

Presto.
Sehr schnell. (stets ganze Takte schlagen.)

poco marc. *cresc.* *f*

47

Bringt den Pro - phe - ten her - aus! Ich möch-te ihn
Bring out the pro - phet. I wish to

cresc.

A. 5503 F.

Sal.
sehn!
see
First soldier.
him Erster Soldat.
Prin - ze - ssin, wir dür - fen nicht
My Prin - cess, we can - not
sfz
sfz
cresc.
ff
(regarding Narraboth)
(erblickt Narraboth) 48
Ah!
Ah!
I. S.
tun, was ihr von uns be - gehrt.
do what you have asked of us.
ff
p
Page.
O, was wird ge - schehn?
What will hap-pen now?
Ich weiss, es wird
I'm sure that some
fp
pp
fpp
poco marc.
pp
(Salome going up to Narraboth)
49 (Salome tritt an Narraboth heran)
Salome
(softly and lively speaking)
(leise und lebhaft sprechend)
Du wirst
You will
Schreck-li-ches ge - schehn.
mis-fortune will happen.
♩. = 76
p
p
marc.

A. 5503 F.

Sal.
das für mich tun, Nar - - - - - - ra-both, nicht wahr?
do this for me, Nar - - - - - ra-both, will you?
tr
dolce
— Ich war dir im - mer ge-wo - gen. Du wirst das für mich
— I have been kind to you e - ver. You will do this for
mf
espressivo
r. H.
50
tun
me.
p
pp
Ich möch-te ihn blos sehn, die-sen
I would but have a look at this
8
selt - - - sa-men Pro - phe - ten.
strange and fo - reign pro - phet
sf
mf
fp
Die Leu - te ha-ben
of whom e - ve - ry
51
so - viel von ihm ge - spro-chen. Ich glau-be, der Tet-rarch hat Angst vor ihm.
bo - dy has been tal-king. The Tetrarch, I believe, is a - fraid of him.
f
tr
A. 5503 F.

Narraboth
52
sempre molto presto
stets äusserst schnell.
Der Tet-rarch hat es aus-drück-lich ver-bo-ten, dass
But the Tetrarch has for-mal-ly for-bid-den that
f
Nar.
ir-gend wer den De-ckel zu die-sem Brun-nen auf-hebt.
a-ny man should raise the co-ver of this cis-tern.
dim.
mf
53 Salome
Du wirst das für mich tun, Nar-ra-both,
You will do this for me, Nar-ra-both.
p
(very hasty)
(sehr hastig)
und mor-gen, wenn ich in ei-ner Sänf-te an dem Tor-weg, wo die
and to-mor-row, when I pass in my lit-ter through the gate-way where the
zart und ausdrucksvoll
pp
Göt-zen-bil-der stehn, vor-bei-kom-me, wer-de ich ei-ne
i-dol-sel-lers sit, when I see you, I shall drop a
(always in a low voice)
(stets sehr leise)
54
grazioso

Sal.
klei-ne Blu - me für dich fal - len las - sen, ein klei - nes
little flow - er, for you I shall drop it, that litt - le
p espr.
Sal.
grü-nes Blüm - chen.
green flow - er.
Narraboth
Prin-ze-ssin, ich kann nicht, ich kann nicht.
My Princess, I can - not, I can - not!
f
f
rfz
(more positive)
(bestimmter) 55
Sal.
Du wirst das für mich tun, Nar -
You'll do this for me, Nar -
f
pp
Sal.
- ra - both. Du weisst, dass du das für mich tun wirst. Und
- ra - both. You know that you will do this thing for me. And to-
mf
p
dim.

A. 5508 F

56

Sal.

mor - gen früh wer - de ich un-ter den Muss' - lin - schlei-ern dir ei - nen Blick zu - wer-fen,
mor - row I will look at you through my mus - lin veils, I shall look at you,

p dolce *p espr.*

Nar - ra-both, ich wer-de dich an-sehn, kann sein,
Nar - ra-both, I shall re - gard you, per-haps,

mf *espr.* *poco f*

57

ich wer - de dir zu - lä - cheln.
e'en I shall be smil - ing at you.

pp

Sieh mich an, Nar - ra - both, sieh mich an. Ah, wie
Look at me, Nar - ra - both. look at me. Ah, you

espr. *cresc.*

A. 5503 I

Sal.
gut du weisst, dass du tun wirst, um was ich dich bit - te.
know that you will do what of you I am ask - ing.
Wie du es weisst!
You know it well...
58
sempre molto presto
Immer äusserst schnell.
(forcibly)
(stark)
Ich weiss, du wirst das
I know that you will
marc.
tun!
do this!
(making a sign to the soldiers)
(gibt den Soldaten ein Zeichen)
Narraboth
Lasst den Pro - phe - ten her - aus - kommen... die Prin - ze - ssin Sa - lo - me
The prophet, let him come forth... for the Princess Sa - lo - mé
cresc.
Nar.
wünscht ihn zu sehn.
wish - es to see him.
59
Ah!
Ah!
Incomminciar abbastanza tranquillo per indi crescere e affrettare fino al Presto.
Etwas ruhig beginnen, doch schnell wieder steigern.
dim.
cresc.
A 5503 F

33
mf molto espr.
cresc.
60
p subito
Ped.
cresc.
f molto espr.
accelerando
cresc.
a tempo
Festes Tempo. rallentando
langsamer als vorher
(feierlich) (solemnly)
acceler.
fp
(solennemente)
pp
Presto
61 Wieder schnell.
f
dim.
Meno mosso
Wieder etwas mässiger.
p
marc.
leggiero
A. 5503 5580 5534 F.

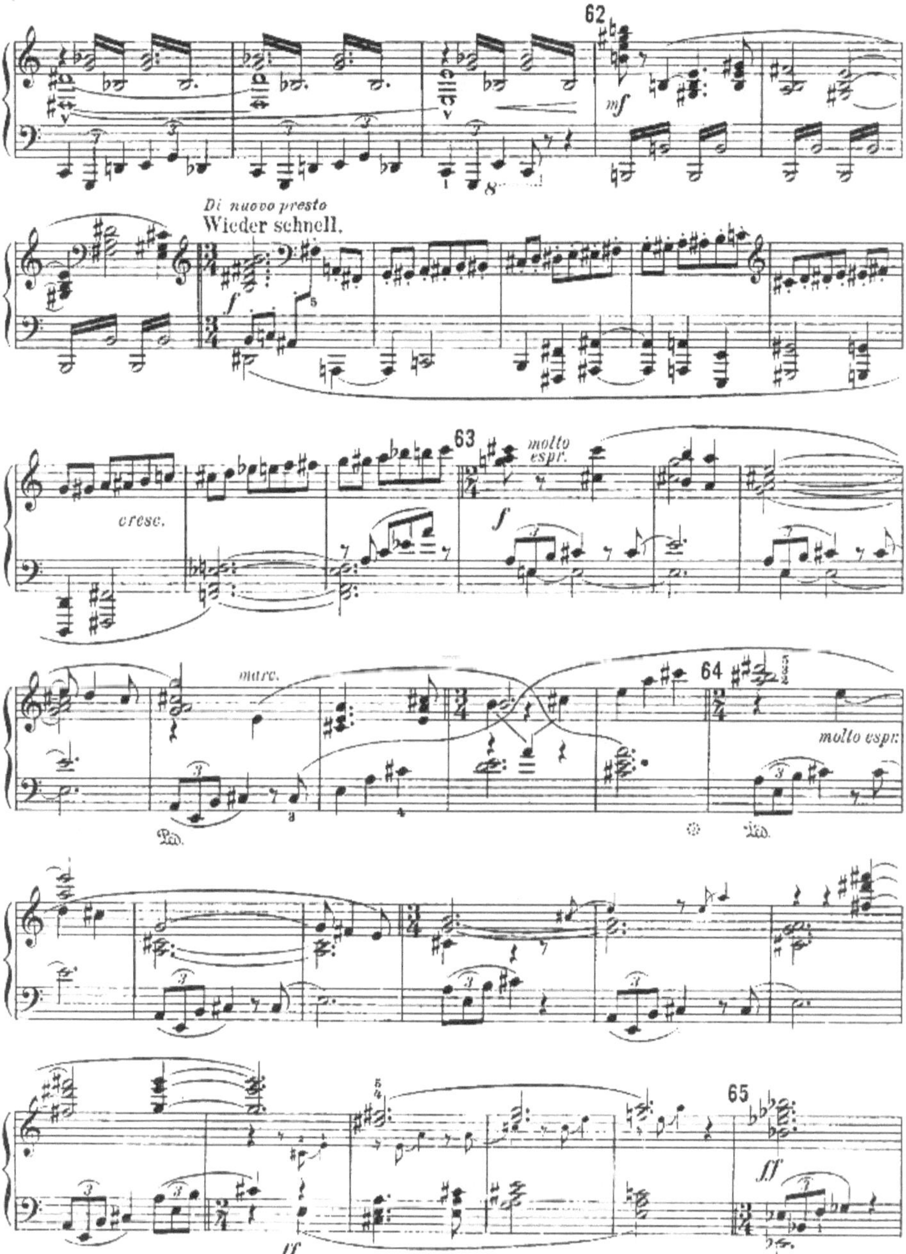

62
mf
Di nuovo presto
Wieder schnell.
f
cresc.
63
molto espr.
f
marc.
Ped.
64
molto espr.
Ped.
ff
65
ff
Ped.

A. 5303 5531 5534 F.

(the prophet comes out of the cistern)
(der Prophet kommt aus der Cisterne)
dim.
Third scene.
Dritte Scene.
Breit. (♩=𝅗𝅥 des 3/4 Metr. ♩=76)
Andante
trem.
(Salomé looks at him and steps slowly back)
(Salome, in seinen Anblick versunken, weicht langsam vor ihm zurück)
L.H.
espr.
66
Jokanaan (with power)
Jochanaan (stark)
Wo ist er, des-sen Sün-den-be-cher jetzt voll ist? Wo ist er, der ei-nes Ta-ges im An-ge-sicht al-les Vol-kes
Where is he with whose sins his cup is fil-lèd? Where is he, who, when his time comes and in the face of all people
Joch.
Jok.
cresc.
mf
A 5503 F

67
Joch.
Jok.
in ei-nem Sil-ber-man-tel ster - ben wird?
shall die wrapped in a robe of sil - - ver?
Heisst ihn
Bid him
cresc.
cresc.
f
her - kom-men, auf dass er die Stim - me Des - sen hö - re,
come for-ward that he may hear the migh - ty voice of him
dim.
mf
ff f
der in der Wü-ste und in den Häusern der Kö - - ni-ge ge - kün - det hat.
who in the de-sert and in the houses of kings has of-ten cried a-loud.
68
fp
cresc.
l. H.
l. H.
l. H.
f
f
f espr.
dim.

A. 5503 F.

69
Poco più mosso
Etwas bewegter.
Salome.
Von wem spricht er?
Of whom is he speaking?
Narraboth.
Nie - mand kann es sa-gen, Prin-zes-sin.
No - bo-dy can tell you, my Princess.
Etwas bewegter.
pp col Ped.
marc.
cresc.
tempo primo
wieder voriges Zeitmass.
Jochanaan.
Jokanaan.
Wo ist sie, die sich hin-gab der Lust ih-rer
Where is she, who succumbed to the lust of her
f
70
Joch.
Jok.
Au - gen, die ge - stan - den hat vor bunt-ge-mal-ten Män-ner -
ey - es, ha - ving seen on the walls the i - ma-ges of pain-ted
mf
sfz
bil - dern und Ge - san-dte in's Land der Chal - dä - - - er
men, and sent am-bas - sa - dors in - to Chal -
sfz

38
71
Salome (low) (tonlos).
Er spricht von mei-ner Mut-ter.
He speaks of my mother.
(impetuous)
Narraboth (heftig).
Nein, nein, Prin-zes-sin.
Oh no, my Princess.
(faint) (matt)
Ja, er
Yes, he
Joch. Jok.
schick-te?
de - a?
poco accel.
pp sfz
mf sfz
ritenuto
wieder breit.
Sal.
spricht von mei - ner Mut-ter.
says that of my mo-ther.
Wo ist sie, die den Hauptleuten Assy-riens sich
Where is she whom the captains of As-sy-ria pos-
gab? Wo ist sie, die sich den jun-gen Män - nern der E-gyp - ter ge-
sessed? Where is she who hath giv'n her-self to the young men of
ff
72
ge - ben hat, die in fei-nen Lei - nen und Hy-a-
E - gypt, who are clothed in li - nen, whose shining
f
mf
pp
p
A. 5503 F.

Joch. / Jok.

cinth - ge-stei-nen pran - gen, de-ren Schil - de von Gold sind und die

hel - mets are of sil - ver, whose shields are of gold and whose

f *f* Ped. Ped.

poco a poco più mosso

73 allmählich bewegter.

Lei - ber wie Rie - - - - sen? Geht, heisst sie

bo - dies are braw - - - - - ny? Go, bid her

mf *appass.* *f*

auf-steh'n vom Bett ih-rer Greu-el, vom Bett ih-rer Blut - schan - -

rise from the bed of her in - cest, the bed of her a - bo - mi - -

f *cresc.*

74

- - de, auf dass sie die Wor - te Des - sen ver - neh - me,

- na - tions, that she may hear the words of the One

pp subito

Joch.
Jok.
der dem Herrn die We - ge be - rei - tet,
who pre - pa - reth the way of the Lord,
molto espressivo
f
accelerando
molto riten.
a tempo
früheres Zeitmass.
75
und ih - re Mis - se - ta - ten be - reu - e. Und wenn sie
and that she may re - pent of her sins. Though she will
ff
gleich nicht be - reut, heisst sie her - kommen, denn die
ne - ver re - pent, bid her come, hear me, for the
sfz
f p
cresc.
76 Salome.
pp
Er ist schrecklich.
He is ter - rible!
Gei - ssel des Herrn ist in sei - ner Hand.
rod of the Lord is in his hand.
Poco più mosso
Etwas bewegter.
dim.
pp

Sal.
Er ist wirk - - lich schreck-lich.
He is ve - - ry ter-ri-ble.
Narraboth.
Bleibt nicht
Do not
espr.
accelerando - - - - - - tempo primo.
Sei-ne Au - gen sind von
It's his eyes a - bove
Nar.
hier, Prin-zes-sin, ich bit-te Euch!
stay here, Prin-cess, I be - seech you.
fp
marc.
77
al-lem das Schrecklichste. Sie sind wie die schwar - zen
all that are ter - ri-ble. They are like the black
mf
pp
Höh - len, wo die Dra-chen hau - sen! Sie
ca - verns, where the dra-gons make their lair! They
marc.
A.5503 F

Sal.
sind wie schwarze Seen, aus de-nen ir-res Mond - licht flak - kert.
are like black lakes from which fantas-tic moons are ris - sing.
78
Sal.
Glaubt ihr, dass er noch ein-mal spre - - chen wird?
Think you, o Nar-ra - both, he will speak a - gain?
accelerando (still more excited)
Narraboth (immer aufgeregter).
Tempo I (non troppo lento).
Früheres Zeitmass (aber nicht zu langsam).
Bleibt nicht hier, Prin-zes-sin, ich bit-te Euch, bleibt nicht hier!
Do not stay here, Princess, I pray of you, do not stay!
espr.
Salome.
Wie ab - - ge - - zehrt er ist! Er ist wie ein
How wast - - ed he is! He's like a thin
Sal.
Bild-niss aus El - - fen - bein. Ge-wiss ist er keusch wie der Mond.
stat - ue of i - - vo - ry. I'm sure he is chaste like the moon.

79
poco a poco più mosso
43
allmählich bewegter.
Sal.
Sein Fleisch muss sehr kühl sein, kühl
His flesh must be cool, cool
espr.
p
pp
wie Elfenbein.
like ivory.
80
Ich möch-
I would
Ped.
accelerando
-te ihn näher beseh'n.
look closer at him.
Ich
I
Narraboth.
Nein, nein, Prinzessin.
No, no, my Princess.
mf
f
muss ihn näher beseh'n.
must look closer at him.
Nar.
Prinzessin, Prinzessin....
Oh, Princess, my Princess!
A. 5503 F.

44
81
Ziemlich bewegt. 𝅗𝅥 = 52, un poco più mosso
Jochanaan. Jokanaan.
Wer ist dies Weib, das mich an - sieht? Ich will ih-re
Who is this wo-man who is looking at me? I'll not have her
Au - gen nicht auf mir ha - ben. Wa - rum sieht sie mich so
eyes rest-ing u-pon me. Where-fore doth she look at
an mit ih-ren Gold-au-gen un-ter den gleissenden Li-
me with her gol-den eyes, un-der her gil-ded eye-
82
dern? Ich weiss nicht, wer sie ist. Ich will nicht
lids? I know not who she is. I do not
wis-sen, wer sie ist. Heisst sie gehn! Zu ihr
wish to know who she is. Bid her go. To her
pp
espr.
cresc.
mf
accelerando

Allegro non troppo
Ziemlich lebhaft.
Salome. 83
Ich bin Sa - - lo -
I am Sa - - - lo -
Joch.
Jok.
will ich nicht spre - chen.
I would not speak.
f
f
pp
Sal.
me, die Tochter der He - ro - di - as, Prin - zes - sin von Ju -
mé, the daughter of He - ro - di - as, the Prin - cess of Ju -
p espr.
Sal.
dä - a.
da - a.
Jochanaan. Jokanaan.
Zu - rück, Toch - ter Ba - by - lons! Komm dem Er -
Stand back! daugh - ter of Ba - by - lon! To the
ff
f
fp
dimin.
Joch.
Jok.
wähl - ten des Herrn nicht na - he! Dei - ne Mut - ter hat die
cho - sen of God ap - proach not! Thy mo - ther hath
84
ff
A 5303 F.

Joch.
Jok.
Er - de er-füllt mit dem Wein ih - rer Lü - ste, und das Un -
fil - led the earth with the wine of her in - i-qui-ties and the cry
sfz
sfz
85
Salome
Sprich mehr, Jo -
Speak again, Jo -
- mass ih-rer Sün - den schreit zu Gott.
of her sins is heard by God.
molto espr.
sfz
fp
f
Sal.
cha - na - an, dei-ne Stim - - me ist wie Mu -
ka - na - an, thy voice is like sweet
sfz
86
sik in mei-nen Oh - ren.
mu - sic to my ears.
p
cresc.

accelerando
tempo primo (agitato)
wieder früheres Zeitmass (bewegt)
Sal.
Sprich mehr, sprich mehr, Jo-
Speak a-gain, speak again, Jo-
Narraboth.
Prin - zessin, Prin - zessin, Prin - zes - - sin.
Oh Prin-cess, my Princess, my Prin - - cess.
wieder früheres Zeitmass (bewegt)
cha - na - an und sag' mir, was ich tun
ka - - na - an, and tell me what to do.
cresc.
87 Molto agitato
Sehr bewegt.
soll?
Jokanaan.
Jochanaan.
Toch - ter So - - doms,
Daugh - ter of So - - dom,
Sehr bewegt.
Joch.
Jok.
komm mir nicht na - he! Viel-mehr be - dek - ke dein Ge -
come ye not near me! Make haste and co - ver thou thy
88

Joch. Jok.
sicht mit ei-nem Schleier, streu-e A - sche auf dei-nen Kopf, mach dich
face with a veil, scat-ter a - shes on thine head, get thee
f sfz mf sfz dim.
89
auf in die Wü-ste und su - che des Men - schen
gone to the de-sert, and seek out the Son of
pp p espr.
Salome.
Wer ist das, des Men-schen Sohn? Ist er so
Who is he, the Son of Man? Is he as
Sohn!
Man.
(zart) pp
Sal.
schön wie du, Jo-cha - - na - an?
beau-ti-ful as thou art, Jo-ka-na - an?
Wei-che von
Get thee
pp f

90
Sal.
Joch.
Jok.
mir! Ich hö - re die Flü - gel des To - des - en - gels im Pa - la - ste
gone! I hear in the pa - lace the beat - ing of the wings of the an - gel of
Jo -
Jo -
dim.
p
dim.
cha - na - an!
ka - na - an!
Narraboth.
Prin - zessin, ich fle - he, geh hin -
My Princess, I beseech thee to go with -
rau - schen....
death.
p
cresc.
Incomminciare un poco più tranquillo
Etwas ruhiger beginnend
91
Jo - cha - na -
Jo - ka - na -
Nar.
ein!
in!
Etwas ruhiger beginnend
f
pp
marc.
p
dim.
A.5503 F.

92
Sal.
an! Ich bin ver-liebt in deinen Leib, Jo-
an! I am am'- rous of thy bo- dy! Jo-
(dolce cantabile)
pp
chana-an! Dein Leib ist weiss wie die Li- lien auf ei-nem
ka-na-an! Thy bo-dy is white, like the li- lies of a wide
Fel-de von der Si-chel nie be-rührt.
field that the mow-er ne-ver hath mowed.
93
Dein Leib ist weiss wie der Schnee auf den Ber-gen Ju-dä-as.
You look as white as the snows on the hills of Ju-dae-a.
p
dim.

A. 5503 F.

Sal.
Die Ro - sen im Gar - - ten von A - ra - biens Kö - - ni - gin
The ro - ses in the gar - - dens of the Queen of A - ra - bi - a
pp espr.
Sal.
sind nicht so weiss wie dein Leib, nicht die
are not so white as thy bo - dy. Nei-ther the
8
pp
94
Sal.
Ro - sen im Gar - ten der Kö - ni - gin, nicht die Fü - sse der Däm - merung auf den
ro - - ses in the gar - dens of A - ra - bia's Queen, nor the feet of the dawn when they light on the
8
pp
espr.
Sal.
Blät - tern, nicht die Brü - ste des Mon - des auf dem Mee - re,
flow - ers nor the breast of the moon on the breast of the o - - cean:
cresc.
8

Sal.
Nichts in der Welt ist so weiss wie dein Leib.
No - thing in this world is so white as thy body.
espr.
ten.
95
(tenderly)
(zart)
Lass mich ihn be - rüh -
Ah, let thy white bo -
p espr.
f espr.
dim.
96
a tempo
ren dei - nen Leib.
dy be touched by me.
Jokanaan.
Jochanaan.
zu-
Stand
smorzando
dim.
calando
a tempo
pp
ff
(with great vivacity)
(sehr lebhaft)
Joch.
Jok.
rück, Toch-ter Ba - by-lons! Durch das Weib kam das U -
back! daugh-ter of Ba - by-lon! For by wo - man came e -
(sehr lebhaft)
f

A. 5503 F.

Joch. Jok.

97

- bel in die Welt. Sprich nicht zu mir.
vil in - to the world. Speak not to me.

p espr.

𝆮 *p*

Ich will dich nicht an - hör'n! Ich hö - re nur auf die
I shall ne - ver listen to thee! I lis - ten but to the

Stim - me des Herrn, mei - nes Got - - - - - tes.
voice of the Lord God Al - migh - - - - ty.

p espr. *pp* *ff*

98 *molto mosso*
Sehr lebhaft.
Salomé.

Dein Leib ist grau - - en - voll. Er ist wie der Leib ei - nes
Thy bo - dy is hi - - - - dious. It's just like the bo - dy of a

dim. *f* *dim.*

A. 5503 F.

Sal.
p
99
Aus - sät - zi - gen. Er ist wie ei - ne ge - tünch - te Wand, wo
le - - per. It is like a plastered wall where
pp
fp
Nat - tern ge - kro - chen sind, wie ei - ne getünch - te Wand, wo Skor -
vi - pers have craw - led; like a plas - tered wall where the
f
100
accelerando
pio - - - - ne ihr Nest ge - baut. Er ist
scor - - - - pions have made their nest. It is
ff
wie ein ü - ber - tünch - tes Grab voll wi - der - li - cher Din - ge. Er ist grässlich.
like a whi - ted se - pul - chre, full of loathsome things. It is hor - rible,
dim.
cresc.

101
poco a poco meno mosso
Wieder ruhiger werden.
Sal.
dein Leib ist gräss - - lich.
thy bo-dy is hor - - - rible.
f
dim.
p
espr.
espr.
dim.
In dein Haar bin ich verliebt, Jo - cha - na-
It's thy hair that I'm en-a - - moured of, Jo - ka - na-
pp
Molto allegro
Schnell.
an. Dein Haar
an. Thy hair
102
ist wie Wein-
is like clus-
dim.
pp
espr.
grazioso

A. 5503 F

56
Sal.
103
trau - - - ben; wie Bü - - - - - - schel schwar -
ters of grapes, like the clus - - - - - - ters of black
p
- - zer Trau - - ben an den Wein - stöcken E - doms.
grapes on the vine - trees of E - dom.
104
Dein Haar ist wie die Ce - - dern, die
Thy hair is like the ce - - dars, the
p espr.
105
gro - ssen Ce - dern von Li - banon, die den Lö - wen und Räu - -
migh - ty ce - dars of Li - banon, that to li - ons and rob - -
Ped. Ped. Ped.
A. 5503 F

106

Sal. bern Schat-ten spen - den. Die lan - - gen schwar -
bars give their shade. The black long

pp

Sal. - zen Näch - te, wenn der Mond sich ver-birgt, wenn die
nights. when the moon hides her face, when the

p

Sal. Ster-ne ban-gen, sind nicht so schwarz, wie dein Haar.
stars are a-fraid, are not so black as thy hair.

f *dim.*

107

Sal. Des Wal - - des Schwei - - gen....
The si - - lence of fo - - rests....

p

A. 5593 F.

Sal.
Nichts in der Welt ist so schwarz wie dein Haar.
No thing in the world is so black as thy hair.
accelerando
f
dimin.
mf
calando Etw. ruhiger.
Meno mosso
108
cresc.
molto espr.
p
pp espr.
Lass mich es be - rüh - ren dein Jokanaan. Haar.
Let me touch thy Jochanaan. hair.
molto tranquillo
sehr ruhig.
dolcissimo
109
Allegro
sehr lebhaft
Zurück, Tochter Sodoms! Be-
Stand back, daugh - ter of So-dom!
ff
f

A. 5503 F.

Joch.
Jok.
rüh - re mich nicht! Entwei - - - - he nicht den Tem - pel des
Touch me not. Profane ye not the tem - ple of the
p
f
espr.
Herrn, mei-nes Got - - tes!
Lord, God Al - migh - - ty.
110
accelerando
(¢)
f (schwungvoll)
Salome.
tempo primo (molto mosso)
wieder früheres Zeitmass (sehr lebhaft)
Dein Haar ist
Thy hair is
ff
sfz
mf
Sal.
gräss-lich! Es starrt von Staub und Un - rat.
hor - ri - ble. With mire and dust it's co - vered.
111
Es ist wie ei-ne
It is just like a
sfz
dim.
f
Dor - nen - kro - ne auf dei-nen Kopf gesetzt. Es ist wie ein
crown of thorns which on thy head is placed. It is like to
112
sfz
dim.
ff

Sal.
Schlan - genkno - ten ge - wik - kelt um dei-nen Hals.
ser - - - pents a - wri - thing round thy neck.
dim.
poco calando
p
113
(with the utmost passion)
(mit höchster Leidenschaft)
Ich lie-be dein Haar nicht. Deinen Mund be -
I love thy hair not. It is thy mouth that
accelerando
pp
f
sfz
geh - - - re ich, Jo - cha - - - na - - an.
I de - sire, Jo - ka - - - na - - an.
espr.
sf
114
Dei-nen Mund be - geh - re ich, Jo - cha - -
It is thy mouth that I de - sire, Jo - ka - -
immer äusserst lebhaft
f
sempre allegro molto

A. 5503 F.

Sal.

- - - na - an. Dein Mund ___ ist wie ein Scharlach-band an ei-nem Turm von
- - - *na - an. Thy mouth ___ is like a band of scar-let on a tow'r of*

fp *dim.* *pp*

115

Sal.

El - fen-bein. Er ist wie ein Gra - nat - - ap - fel, von ei-nem Sil - ber-
i - vo - ry. It is like a sweet pome - gra - nate cut with a knife of

pp

116

Sal.

mes-ser zer-teilt. Die Gra - nat - ap-fel-blü - ten in den Gär - ten von Ty - rus,
i - vo - ry. Ah, the pome-granate flow-ers that blos - som at Tyre, and are

p

Sal.

glüh-en - der als Ro - - - - - sen, sind nicht so rot. Die
red - der than ro - - - - - ses, are not so red. The red

cresc. *f*

A 5503 F

117
Sal.
ro - ten Fan-fa-ren der Trom-pe - ten, die das Nah'n von Kön' - - gen kün-den
blasts of the trum-pets that he - rald the ap-proach of kings - - in war-time
p
p
molto espr.
Sal.
und vor de-nen der Feind er-zit - tert, sind nicht so rot
and that fill with fear the en' - my, are not so red
f
Sal.
wie dein ro-ter Mund.
as thy thin red mouth.
118
Dein Mund ist rö - - -
Thy mouth is red - - -
dim.
p
espr.
pp
Sal.
- ter als die Fü-sse der Män - - ner, die den Wein stampfen in der
- der than the feet of the men who tread the wine, stamping in the
espr.
Ped.
A 5503 F

Sal.
119
Kel-ter. Er ist rö - - - ter als die Füs-se der Tau-ben, die in den
wine-press. It is red - - - der than the feet of the doves who haunt the
pp
Tem - peln wohnen. Dein Mund ist wie ein Ko - ral - lenzweig in der
ho - ly tem-ples. Thy mouth is like a branch of co - ral found in the
molto stringendo
mit grosser Steigerung
pespr. cresc.
fp
120
Dämm'rung des Meers, wie der Pur - - - - pur in den Gru-ben von Mo - ab,
twi-light of the sea; like ver - mi - - - lion in the mines of far Mo - ab,
cresc.
(beside herself)
(ausser sich)
121
der Purpur der Kö - - - - ni - ge.... nichts in der Welt
ver-mi-lion that kings would take... no-thing in the world
fp
cresc.
ff
A. 5503 F.

Sal.
ist so rot wie dein Mund. Lass
is so red as thy mouth. Ah,
8
marc. dim.
p
calando
122 ruhiger werden
dim.
molto ritard.
meno mosso
pp langsamer
mich ihn küs - sen dei - nen Mund.
let me kiss thy mouth, kiss thy mouth.
Jochanaan (leise, in tonlosem Schauder)
Jokanaan (low in soundless horror) Nie-mals,
Ne - ver!
ruhiger werden
langsamer
sfz
ppp
pp
8va bassa
Joch. Jok.
Toch-ter Ba-by-lons, Toch-ter So - doms... Niemals!
Daughter of Ba - by - lon! Daughter of So - dom! Ne - ver!
mf
Salome. Allegro molto
wieder sehr lebhaft
Ich will dei-nen Mund küs - sen. Jo - cha - na - an.
O let me kiss thy mouth, Jo - ka - na - an.
(molto appassionato)
f
A. 5508 F.

123
Sal.
Ich will dei-nen Mund küs - sen
O let me kiss thy mouth!
Narraboth (in höchster Angst und Verzweiflung)
(in greatest anguish and despair)
Prinzes-sin, Prin-zes - sin, die
O Princess, my Prin - cess, who
ff
Nar.
wie ein Gar - ten von Myr-rhen ist, die die Tau - be aller Tau - ben ist,
art like a gar - den of sweet - est myrrh, who art the dove of all the do - ves,
p espr.
pp
mf
124
Nar.
sieh diesen Mann nicht an. Sprich nicht sol - che Wor - te zu ihm.
look not at this man. Do not speak such words to him.
accelerando
marc.
espr.
f
125
Salome.
Ich will dei-nen Mund
O let me kiss
Nar.
Ich kann es nicht er - tra - gen....
I can - - - not bear to hear them....
ff
mf

126
Sal.
küs - sen. Jo - cha - na - an
thy mouth, Jo - ka - na - an.
Ich will dei - nen
O let me
cresc.
12
Sehr schnell.
Allegrissimo
Mund küs - sen
kiss thy mouth
(Narraboth ersticht sich und fällt tot zwischen Salome und Jochanaan.)
(Narraboth kills himself and falls between Salome and Jokanaan.)
fff
ff
127
Lass mich dei - nen Mund küs -
O let me kiss thy
p
espr.
mf
sen, Jo - cha - na - an.
mouth, Jo - ka - na - an.
cresc.
f
sf
mf
128
A. 5503 F.

Jokanaan.
Jochanaan.
Wird dir nicht ban - ge, Toch-ter der He - -
Art thou not fright - ened, daughter of He - -
f
mf
129 Salomé.
Lass mich dei-nen Mund küs - sen, Jo - cha - na-an!
O — let me kiss thy mouth, Jo - ka - na-an!
Joch.
Jok.
ro - di - as? Toch - ter der
ro - di - as? Daugh - ter of a -
appassionato
sf
f
130
Un - - - zucht, es lebt nur Ei-ner, der dich ret - - ten
dul - - - te - ry, there is but one who can save
espr
p
cresc.
131
kann. Geh, such' ihn. Such'
thee. poco meno mosso Go, seek Him. molto agitato Seek
Etwas breit.
wieder sehr bewegt
espr.
fp

(fervently)
(mit grösster Wärme)
132
Joch.
Jok.
ihn! Er ist in ei-nem Na - - chen
Him! He is in a boat
sempre alla breve
(singend) (singing)
dim.
p
col Ped.
auf dem See von Ga-li-lä - - - - - a
on the sea of Ga-li-lae - - - - - a
und re - - - - det zu sei-nen Jün - - gern.
and tal - - - - keth with his dis-cip - - les.
(most solemnly)
(sehr feierlich)
133
Knie nie-der am U - - fer des Sees, ruf ihn
Kneel down on the shore of the sea, and call unto
pp espr.

Joch. Jok.

an. Und ru - fe ihn beim
Him. And call to Him His

espr.
p

134

Joch. Jok.

Na - - - - - men. Wenn er zu dir kommt,
ho - - ly name. When He com - èth,

ff
f molto espr.
dim.
p

Joch. Jok.

und er kommt zu al - len, die ihn ru - fen, dann bük - ke dich
(and to all who call on Him He com - èth) then bow thy-self

pp
dim.
pp espr.

135

Joch. Jok.

zu sei - nen Fü - ssen, dass er dir
at His feet and ask of Him

cresc.
fp

Jokanaan.
139 Jochanaan.
Ich will dich nicht an-sehn. Du bist ver-flucht, Sa-
I will not__ see thee. Thou art ac-cursed, Sa-
sfz p
Joch.
Jok.
- - - lo-me. Du bist ver-flucht.
- - - lo-me. Thou art ac-cursed.
cresc.
ff
140
Du bist ver-flucht.
Thou art ac-cursed!
molto accelerando
sf
f
ff
Du bist__ ver-
Thou art__ ac-
sfz

A. 5503 F.

A. 5503 5530 5534 F.

tempo primo
wieder früheres Zeitmass
143
accelerando
Molto mosso
Sehr lebhaft.
144

75
molto appassionato
immer schneller
più allegro
145
146
A. 5503 6530 5534 F.

fff

marc. 147

m. d.

sfz

148

accelerando

sfz dim.

sfz

cresc.

Ped.

poco ritenuto

a tempo (allegro molto) (sehr schnell)

fff

mf

Ped.

ff

149

calando

p

molto cresc.

ff dim.

Ped.

150 Molto più tranquillo
Viel ruhiger.

p f

mf

Allegro molto
wieder sehr schnell

p

cresc.

Ped.

A. 5503 5530 5534 F.

151
Andante. ♩ = 𝅗𝅥 del ¢
Beinahe doppelt so langsam.
dim.
ppp
152
cresc.
dim.
153
sfz pp

154

Vierte Scene. Fourth scene.

Etwas lebhafter.

un poco più mosso

cresc.

accelerando

cresc.

Allegro

155 Schnell. M. 𝅗𝅥 = 66

(Herodes tritt rasch ein, gefolgt von Herodias)

(Herod enters hastily, followed by Herodias.)

Herod.
Herodes.

Wo ist Sa - lo - me?
Where is Sa - lo - me?

Wo ist die Prinzes - sin?
Where is the__ Prin - cess?

Herodes

Warum kam sie nicht wieder zum Ban - kett, wie ich ihr befoh - len hat - te?
Why did she not re - turn to__ the banquet as I__ comman - ded her?

cresc.

A. 5503 F.

156
Herodes
Ah! — da ist sie!
Ah! — there she is!
espr.
ff
ffp
dim.
Herodias.
Du sollst sie nicht an - sehn.
You must not — look at her.
pp mf
p
Herodias
Fort-während siehst du sie an!
You're always look - ing at her!
Herod.
Herodes.
Wie der
Ah, the
espr.
pp
157
Herodes
Mond heu-te Nacht aus-sieht!
moon look-eth strange to - night!
Ist es nicht ein selt - sa-mes
Is she not — hav - ing a
mf
pp
A. 5503 F.

Herodes

Bild? Es sieht aus, wie ein wahn - wit-zi-ges
strange look? She is like a mad wo - man, a mad

cresc.

Herodes

Weib, das ü-ber-all nach Buh-len sucht....
wo - man who seeks for lo-vers e-v'ry-where.

espr.

l. H.

158

accelerando

Herodes

wie ein betrun-kenes Weib, das durch
Much like a drun-ken wo - man that is

cresc.

Herodias.

Tempo primo
früheres Zeitmass

Nein, der Mond ist wie der
No; the moon is like the

Herodes

Wol - ken tau - melt....
reel - ing through the clouds.

früheres Zeitmass

Herodias
Herodes
Mond, das ist al - les. Wir wol - len hin - ein - gehn.
moon, that is all. Let us go in a - gain.
Ich will
I will
fp
fp
p
159
hier - blei - ben. Mannas-sah, leg Teppi-che hieher! Zün - det
stay out here! Ma-nas-seh, lay car - pets here! Light up
p
cresc.
Fak - keln an! Ich will noch Wein mit mei - nen Gä - sten
tor - ches! I will drink more wine with my guests. Bring
cresc.
p
160
Allegro molto
Sehr schnell. Metr. 𝅗𝅥 = 80.
trin - ken
ta - bles.
Ah
Ah
ff

Herodes
Ich bin aus - ge-glit - ten.
I have slip - - pèd!
mf
dim.
pp
Ich bin in Blut ge - tre - ten, das ist ein bö - ses Zei - chen.
Ah, in blood I have slip-pèd, it is an ill o - men.
161
Die Viertel immer gleich.
Wa - rum ist hier Blut? Und dieser
Where-fore is there blood? and this
Ped.
To - te? Wer ist die - ser To - te hier? Wer
bo - dy? What does this bo - dy here? Who

Herodes
ist die-ser To-te? Ich will ihn nicht sehn.
is this dead man? I will not look on him.

First Soldier.
Erster Soldat.
Es ist unser Hauptmann,
It is our cap-tain,

poco f
sfz
dim.
pp

162

Herodes
Ich er-liess kei-nen Be-fehl, dass er ge-tö-tet wer-de.
'Twas not I who gave the or-der that he should be killed.

1. S.
Herr. Er hat sich
sire. He hath

f (wild)
(ferociously)
f

Herodes
Das scheint mir selt-sam. Der jun-ge
And for what rea-son? This young

1. S.
selbst ge-tö-tet, Herr.
kil-led him-self, sire.

tranquillo
p
pp
pp

Herodes
Sy-rier, er war sehr schön. Ich er-
Sy-rian was ve-ry fair. I re-

pp

A. 5503 F.

163
Hero-des
inn-re mich,
member now.
ich sah sei-ne schmachtenden Au-
I saw that he look-ed lan-guor-
pp espr.
p
-gen, wenn er Sa-lo-me an-sah.
ous-ly at Sa-lo-mé, I saw it.
M.
Fort mit
Off with
pp
ff
164 (They take away the body)
(Sie tragen den Leichnam weg)
ihm.
him.
Es ist
It is
kalt hier.
cold here.
accelerando
Es
There
pp
cresc.
weht ein Wind....
blows a wind....
f

Tempo primo
Früheres Zeitmass.
Herodias.
(drily)
(trocken)
165
Nein, es weht kein Wind.
No, there is no wind.
Herodes
Weht nicht ein Wind? Ich
Blows there no wind? I
Früheres Zeitmass.
dim.
fp
pp
accelerando
sa - ge Euch: es weht ein
tell you: there is a
p
accelerando
cresc.
Wind, und in der Luft
wind, and in the air
dim.
f
166
hör ich et - was, wie das Rau
I hear some - thing like the beat
p
A. 5503 F.

sempre accelerando
Herodes
sehen von mächt - gen Flü - geln...
ing of vast wings.
cresc.
dim.
Tempo primo
Früheres Zeitmass.
Herodias.
Ich hö - re nichts
I hear no-thing.
Herodes
Hört ihr es nicht?
Do you not hear?
Jetzt hö - re ich es
Now I can hear it no
Früheres Zeitmass.
167
un poco più tranquillo
Etwas ruhiger.
Herodes
nicht mehr. A - ber ich ha - be es ge - hört, es
lon - ger. But I did hear it, It

A. 5508 F.

168
più mosso
Wieder schneller.
Herodes
war das Wehn des Win-des. Es ist vor - ü - ber.
was the blow - ing of winds. It is now o - ver.
dim.
pp
Horch! Hört Ihr es nicht?
Hark! Do you not hear it?
Das
The
cresc.
f
dim.
169
Rau - schen von mächt - gen Flü - geln...
beat - ing of vast wings.
cresc.
mf
mar.

Herodias
Du bist krank, wir wol-len hin-
You are ill. Let's go with-
cresc.
ff
mf
fp
f
170
Herodias
ein gehn.
in.
Herodes
Ich bin nicht krank,
I am not ill.
p
cresc.
f
Herodes
a-ber dei-ne Toch-ter ist krank zu To-de
It is your daugh-ter who's sick to death.
171
sfz espressivo
Herodias
Ich
I
Herodes
Nie-mals hab ich sie so blass ge-sehn
Ne-ver have I seen her look-ing so pale.
dim.
p
pp

A. 5503 F

172
Herodias
ha-be dir. ge-sagt, du sollst sie nicht an-sehn.
have told— you, you should not re-gard her.
Herodes
Schenkt mir Wein ein!
Pour out wine for me!
accelerando
f sfz
f p
cresc.
f
Sehr lebhaft. M. 𝅗𝅥.=80
Sa - lo-me, komm. trink Wein mit
Sa - lo-mé, come drink wine with
mir. ei-nen köst - li-chen Wein.
me, this is ex - qui-site wine.

90
173
Herodes
Cä - sar selbst hat ihn mir ge-schickt.
Wine that Cae - - - - - sar sent me him-self.
f
dim.
tr
p
Tauche dei-ne klei-nen Lip-pen hin-ein.
Pray, dip in-to it thy lit-tle red lips.
174
marc.
Dei-ne klei-nen ro-ten Lip-pen, dann will ich den Be-cher lee-ren.
Ah! such lit-tle bright red lips, then I will drain the cup.
175
Salomé
Ich bin nicht durstig, Te-
I am not thirsty, Te-
pp
dim.

Sal.
trarch.
trarch.
Herodes
Hörst du, wie sie mir ant-wor-tet,
Hear now, how she doth ans-wer me,
die-se dei-ne Toch-ter?
this daughter of yours?
sfz p
sempre molto vivace
Herodias.
176 Immer sehr lebhaft.
Sie hat Recht. War-um starrst du sie im-mer an.
She does right. Why are you al-ways ga-zing at her?
Herodes
Bringt rei-fe Früch-te!
Bring me ripe fruits!
fp
sf
f
Metr. 𝅗𝅥=88.
Herodes
Sa-lo-me komm,
Sa-lo-mé, come,
cresc.
f
mf
Herodes
iss mit mir von die-sen Früch-ten.
eat with me some of these fruits.
177
dim.
p

Herodes
Den Ab - druck dei - - ner klei - nen weis - sen
I love to see thy litt - le shi - ning
sfz
pp
Herodes
Zäh - - ne in ei - ner Frucht seh' ich so
teeth and their pret - ty marks in a sweet
pp
f
dim.
Herodes
178
gern.
fruit.
p
pp
Herodes
Beiss nur ein we - nig ab. Nur ein we - nig
Bite but a lit - tle bit, but a litt - tle
p

A. 5503 F.

Herodes
179
von die - ser Frucht dann
of this sweet fruit then
cresc.
f
Salomé
Ich bin nicht
I am not
Herodes
will ich es - sen, was ü - brig ist.
I will eat what is left for me.
dim.
pp
180
Sal.
hung - rig, Te - trarch.
hun - gry, Te - trarch.
Herodes
Du siehst, wie du die - se dei - ne
You see how you have brought up this
Herodias
Mei - ne Toch - ter und ich stam - men aus
My daugh - ter and I come of a
Herodes
Toch - ter er - zo - gen hast!
daughter of yours, you see!
cresc.
A. 5508 F.

Herodias

181

kö-nig-li-chem Blut. Dein Va-ter war Ka-meel-trei-ber, dein Va-ter war ein
ro-yal race. Thy fa-ther was a camel dri-ver! Thy fa-ther was a

Herodias

poco meno mosso
Etwas ruhiger.

Dieb und ein Räu-ber o-ben drein.
thief and a rob-ber al-so.

Herodes Herod.

Sa-lo-me,
Sa-lo-mé,

dim.

Herodes

più 182 vivo
wieder lebhafter werden.

komm, setz dich zu mir. Du sollst auf dem
come, sit next to me. I will give thee the

Herodes

183

Thron dei-ner Mut-ter sit-zen.
throne of thy mo-ther to sit u-pon.

Meno
Viel

A. 5503 E.

Salomé
Ich bin nicht müde, Tetrarch.
I am not ti-rèd, Te-trarch.
Herodias
Du siehst, wie sie dich achtet.
You see what she thinks of you.
mosso
ruhiger
cresc.
Più vivo
Lebhafter.
Herodes
Bringt mir — was wünsche ich denn?
Bring me — what is't that I desire?
mf
dim.
184
Ich habe es vergessen. Ah! Ah! Ich erinnre mich—
I forgot all about it. Ah! Ah! I remember now—
accelerando
cresc.
Moderato
Mässig langsam. M. 𝅗𝅥 = 60
Stimme des Jochanaan
The Voice of Jokanaan
Sieh, die Zeit ist gekommen,
Lo! the time is come now,
fpp

185
Joch.
Jok.
der Tag, von dem ich sprach, ist da.
the day, of which I spoke is there.
fp
pp
186
Lebhafter.
Herodias
Heiss' ihn schweigen! Dieser Mensch be-schimpft mich!
Bid him be si-lent! This man is in-sult-ing me!
più mosso
Herod.
Herodes.
Er hat
He has
Lebhafter.
f
Äusserst lebhaft.
Hero-dias.
Molto mosso
Ich glaube nicht an Pro-
I do not be-lieve in
Hero-des.
nichts gegen dich gesagt. Ü-ber-dies ist er ein sehr grosser Pro-phet.
said no-thing against you. Besides, he is a ve-ry great prophet.
Äusserst lebhaft.
fp
sempre più mosso
187 Immer schneller.
phe-ten. A-ber du, du hast Angst vor ihm!
pro-phets. I know well you are a-fraid of him!
Ich ha-be vor
I am a-
Immer schneller.
f
ten.

Herodias. Ich sa-ge dir, du hast Angst vor ihm. Wa-rum
I tell you, you are a-fraid of him. Why

Herodes. nie-mandem Angst.
fraid of no man.

Herodias. lie-ferst du ihn nicht den Ju-den aus, die seit Mo-na-ten nach ihm schrei-en?
do you not de-li-ver him to the Jews, who these six months have been clam'ring for him?

1st Jew. 1. Jude. Wahr-
Tru-

188 *Molto allegro*
Schnell, in wechselnder Taktart ♩ stets gleich ♩

1. Jude. haf-tig, Herr, es wä-re bes-ser, ihn in un-sre Hän-de zu ge-ben!
ly, my lord, it were much bet-ter to de-li-ver him in-to our hands.

Herod. Herodes. Ge-
E-

Schnell, in wechselnder Taktart ♩ stets gleich ♩

Herodes. nug da-von! Ich wer-de ihn nicht in eu-re Hän-de ge-ben. Er ist ein
nough of this! I have al-rea-dy giv'n my ans-wer to you. He is a

Molto allegro
Sehr schnell. M. ♩. = 120.
Herodes.
heil-ger Mann. Er ist ein Mann, der Gott ge-schaut hat.
ho-ly man. He is a man by whom God has been seen.
1st Jew.
1. Jude.
Das kann nicht sein.
That can-not be.
Sehr schnell. M. ♩. = 120.
pp
fz
Ped.
1. Jude.
Seit dem Pro-phe-ten E - li-as hat nie - mand Gott ge-
Since the great pro-phet E - li-as no man hath seen Lord
poco f
189
1. Jude.
sehn. Er war der letz - te, der Gott von
God. He is the last man who hath seen
f marc.
p
1. Jude.
An-gesicht ge-schaut. In un-sern Ta-gen zeigt sich Gott nicht. Gott ver-
God face to face. In these our days God doth not show Him-self. God is
dim
f

190

1. Jude.

birgt sich. Da-rum ist gro-sses Ü-bel ü-ber das Land ge-kom-men
hi-ding Him-self. Therefore great evils have come u-pon the coun-try.

mf

gro-sses Ü-bel.
great evils.

2nd Jew.
2. Jude.

In Wahrheit weiss nie-mand, ob E-li-as in der Tat
And ve-ri-ly, no man doth know if E-li-as

p *fp*

2. Jude.

Gott ge-se-hen hat. 191 Mög-li-cher-wei-se war es nur der Schat-ten
e-ver saw the Lord. Per-ad-ven-ture it was but the sha-dow of

dim. *pp*

2. Jude.

Got-tes, was er sah. 192
God that he saw.

3rd Jew.
3. Jude.

Gott ist zu kei-ner Zeit ver-bor-gen.
God is at no time hid-den

f *p* *p* *f marc.*

3. Jude.
Er zeigt sich zu al - len Zei-ten und an al - len Or - ten. Gott
He show-eth Him-self at all times and in e - - v'rything. God
— ist im schlim - men e - ben-so wie im gu - - ten.
— is in what is good and in what is e - vil.
193
4. Jude.
4th Jew.
Du sollt-est das nicht
Thou shouldst not say such
sa-gen, es ist ei-ne sehr ge-fähr-li-che Leh - re aus A - le -
things. It is a ve-ry dan - ge-rous doc-trine that co - meth from A - le -
xan - dri - a. Und die Grie - chen sind Hei - - - den.
xan - dri - a. And the Greeks are Gen - - - - tiles.
194
5. Jude.
5th Jew.
Nie - mand kann sa-gen, wie
No man can tell us how
mf
p
f
cresc.
A 5503 F.

5. Jude.
Gott wirkt. Sei-ne We-ge sind sehr dun - kel. Wir
God wor-këth. His ways are ve-ry mys-te - ri-ous.
dim.
pp
p
5. Jude.
könnnen nur un-ser Haupt un-ter sei - nen Wil - len beu - - - gen, denn
We must needs sub - mit to all and e - v'ry-thing. for
195
1st Jew.
1. Jude.
Du sagst die Wahr - - - - - heit. Für-
Thou speak-est tru - - - - - ly. Oh
5 Jude.
Gott ist sehr stark.
God is ve - ry strong.
mf
f p
1 Jude.
wahr, Gott ist furcht - - - - - - bar, A-ber was
yes. God is ter - - - - - - rible. Of this man
f subito

196
1. Jude.
die-sen Menschen an-geht, der hat Gott nie ge-sehn. Seit dem Pro-pheten E-li-as hat
thought it is quite certain, he hath ne-ver seen God. Since the prophet E-li-as
ff
fp
1. Jude.
nie-mand Gott ge-sehn.
no man hath seen the Lord.
197
2. Jude.
2nd Jew.
In Wahr-heit weiss nie-mand,
In-deed, no man knoweth
f
mf
1. Jude.
Er war der letz-te, er war der letz-
He is the last man, he is the last
2. Jude.
ob E-li-as in der Tat Gott ge-
if the pro-phet E-li-as did
sfz p
198
1. Jude.
-te, der Gott von An-ge-sicht zu
man, E-li-as is the last man
2. Jude.
se-hen hat. Gott ge-se-hen hat.
see the Lord. God was seen by him.
3rd Jew.
3. Jude.
mf
Gott ist zu kei-ner
God is at no
p
marc.
sfz p

1. Jude.
An - ge-sicht ge-schaut. In un- - sern Ta - gen zeigt sich Gott nicht. Gott ver-
who saw God our Lord. In these days God doth not show Him-self God
2. Jude.
3. Jude.
Zeit ver-bor- - - - - gen. Er
time hid- - - - - den. He
4. Jude. (zum dritten)
4th Jew (to the third)
Du soll-test das nicht sa - gen.
This is a dang'-rous doc - trine.
marc.
199
birgt sich.
hi - - - - - dèth Himself.
Gott ver-
God is
Mög-li - cher-wei - se war es nur der Schat - ten,
Per - ad-ven - ture it was but the sha - dow,
zeigt sich zu al - - - - - - len Zei - - - - - ten
show - èth Him - self at all times.
Es ist ei - ne sehr ge - fähr-li - che
'Tis a dang'-rous doc - trine that comes from the
f marc.
dim.

A. 5503 F.

1. Jude.
birgt sich. Da-rum ist gro-sses Ü-bel
hid - - - - - - ing Him-self. There-fore great evils
2. Jude.
mög-li-cher-wei-se mög-li-cher-wei-se war es nur der Schat-ten
per-ad-ven-ture, per-ad-ven-ture it was but the sha-dow of
3. Jude.
4. Jude.
Leh-re aus A-le-xan-dri-a. Und die Grie-chen sind
schools of A-le-xan-dri-a. And the Greeks are
200
1. Jude.
ü-ber das Land ge-kom-men. Darum ist gro-sses Ü-bel
have come up-on the coun-try. Therefore great evils
2. Jude.
Got-tes, was er sah.
God that he saw.
3. Jude.
Er zeigt sich an al-len Or-ten.
He show-eth Him-self in all things.
4. Jude.
Hei-den. Sie sind nicht einmal be-schnit-ten.
Gen-tiles. They are not e-ven cir-cum-cised.
5. Jude.
5th Jew. Nie-mand kann sa-gen, wie Gott
No one can tell us how God
cresc.

Von *) ab sind die Solostimmen nach dem Ermessen des Dirigenten durch einige tüchtige Chorsänger zu verstärken.
*From the *) the solo singers may be reinforced by a number of good chorus singers at the discretion of the conductor.*

A. 5503 F.

201
1. Jude.
letz - - - - - - - - -te, der Gott von An - ge - sicht zu
last one of all the pro - phets who did
2. Jude.
se - hen hat.
saw the Lord.
3. Jude.
ff
Gott ist zu kei - ner Zeit ver -
God is at no time
4. Jude.
ff
Nie - mand kann
No man can
5. Jude.
ff
Nie - mand kann sa - - gen, wie Gott wirkt
No one can tell us how God work - eth
cresc.
202
An - gesicht ge - schaut.
see the face of God.
Es war der letz - - te, der
He was the last one of
Gott ist furcht - - - - bar, er
God is ter - - - - - ri - ble, he
bor - - - - gen.
hid - - - - den.
sa - gen, wie Gott wirkt, denn Gott ist sehr stark.
tell us how God workèth, for God is ve - ry strong.
sei - ne We - ge sind sehr dun - - kel.
and his ways are ve - ry mys - te - ri - ous.
marcatissimo

A. 5503 F.

1. Jude.
2. Jude.
3. Jude.
4. Jude.
5. Jude.
Gott von An - gesicht zu An - ge-sicht ge - schaut,
all the pro - - phets who saw the face of God,
bricht den Star - - ken in Stük - - ke, den
break-eth the strong one to pie - - ces, the
Gott ist zu
God is at
Nie - mand kann sa - gen, wie Gott
No one can tell us how God
Es kann sein, dass die Din - ge, die wir gut nen - nen, sehr
It may be that the things which we call good are ve - ry
203
er war der letz-te, der Gott von An - ge-sicht zu An - ge-sicht ge -
he was the last one of all, of all the prophets who saw the face of
Star - ken wie den Schwachen, denn je-der gilt ihm gleich.
strong alike the weak, to Him we're all a - like.
kei - ner Zeit ver - bor - gen. Gott zeigt sich zu
no time hid - den. God sho-weth him -
wirkt.
work - - èth.
Gott ist sehr
God is quite
schlimm sind, und die Din-ge, die wir schlimm nen - nen.
e - vil, and the things which we call e - - vil

1. Jude.
schaut. Er war der letz - te, der Gott von
God. He is the last one of all the
3. Jude.
al - len Zei - ten und an al - len Or - ten.
self at all times and in e - v'ry-thing.
(allein) (alone)
Gott ist im gu - ten
God's in the good as
4. Jude.
stark. Er bricht der Star - ken wie den Schwa - - chen in Stük - ke
strong. He breaketh the strong as well as the weak ones to pie - ces.
5. Jude.
sehr gut sind. Wir wis - sen von nichts et - was.
may be good. There's no knowledge of a - ny-thing.
Herodias
(to Herod) (zu Herodes).
204
(bursting out) (heftig)
Heiss sie schwei - - - - gen,
Bid them be si - - - - - lent,
1. Jude.
An - ge - sicht zu An - ge - sicht ge - schaut.
pro - phets, who has seen the face of God.
2. Jude.
(allein) (alone)
Mög - li - cher - wei - se
Per - ad - ven - ture
3. Jude.
e - ben - so wie im bö - - sen....
well as in the e - - vil.
4. Jude.
(allein) (alone)
Gott ist stark
God is strong...
5. Jude.
(alone) (allein)
Wir wis - sen von nichts et - was, von nichts et - was....
There's no knowledge of a - ny - thing, of a - ny - thing....

A. 5503 F.

Herodias.
sie lang - - wei - len mich.
They wea - - - - ry me.
Herodes.
Herod. Doch hab ich da - von spre - chen hö - ren, Jo - cha - na -
But I have heard it some - times said that Jo - ka - na -
2. Jude.
war es nur der Schat - ten Got - - tes.
it was but the sha - dow of God.
sfz
poco f
Herodes.
an sei in Wahr - heit eu - er Pro - phet E - li - as.
an him - self is your prophet E - li - as.
205
1. Jude (allein).
1st Jew (alone) Das kann nicht sein, seit den
That can - not be, since the
p
mf
1. Jude.
Ta - gen des Pro - phe - ten E - li - - - - - as sind mehr als drei - hun - dert
days of the pro - phet E - li - - - - - as more than three hundred
sfz

A. 5503 F.

206
1. Jude.
Jah-re ver-gangen.
years have e-lap-sed.
2nd Jew.
2. Jude.
Das kann nicht
That can-not
3rd Jew.
3. Jude.
Kei-nes-wegs,
Not at all,
Kei-neswegs, er ist
Not at all, he is
1st Nazarene
1. Nazarener.
Mir ist si-cher, dass er der Pro-phet E-li-as ist.
I am sure that he is the prophet E-li-as.
fp
fz
sein. Seit den Ta-gen des Pro-phe-ten E-li-
be. Since the days of the pro-phet E-li-
er ist nicht der Pro-phet E-li-
he is ne-ver the pro-phet E-li-
nicht der Pro-phet E-li-as.
ne-ver the pro-phet E-li-as.
4. Jude.
4th Jew.
Kei-nes-wegs,
Not at all,
5th Jew.
5. Jude.
Kei-nes-wegs,
Not at all,
er ist nicht der Pro-phet E-
he is ne-ver the pro-phet E-

Herodias.
Heiss sie schwei - - - - - - - -
Bid them si - - - - - - - -
1. Jude.
- - - as sind mehr als drei - hun - dert Jah - re ver - gan - gen...
- - - as more than three hun - dert years are gone..
2. Jude.
as.
as.
4. Jude.
er ist nicht der Pro - phet E - li - - - - - - - as.
he is ne - ver the pro - phet E - li - - - - - - - as.
5. Jude.
li - - - - - as.
li - - - - - as.
207
Herodias.
- gen!
- lence!
Stimme des Jochanaan.
The Voice of Jokanaan.
Sie - he, der Tag ist na - he, der Tag des Herrn,
So the day is come, the day of God
M. 𝅗𝅥. = 66. (𝅗𝅥. etwas ruhiger als vorher 𝅗𝅥.) (𝅗𝅥. somewhat quieter than the preceding 𝅗𝅥.)
f pp
Joch. Jok.
und ich hö - re auf den Ber - gen die Schrit - te Des - sen, der sein
and I hear u - pon the mountains the feet of Him who shall
ben 208 sostenuto
sehr getragen
pp
espr.

112
Herod.
Herodes. p
Was soll das heissen,
What does that mean,
Joh.
wird der Er- lö- ser der Welt.
be the Sa- viour of the world.
pp
Hero-des.
der Er- lö- ser der Welt?
the Sa-viour of the world?
209
1st Nazarene (emphatically)
1. Nazarener (emphatisch).
Der Mes- si- as ist ge-
The Mes- si- ah is now
pespr.
f
1st Jew (screaming)
1. Jude (schreiend).
Der Mes-si-as ist nicht ge-kommen.
The Mes-si-ah is not yet come.
1. Naz.
kom- men. Er ist ge- kom- men, und al-
come. Yes, he is come now, working mi-
dim.
p
espr.
210
(sehr ruhig) very quietly
lent- hal-ben tut er Wun- der. Bei ei- ner
ra- cles where He pass- eth. Thus, at a
dim.
pp
A. 5503 F.

1. Naz.
Hochzeit in Ga-li-lä - a hat er Was-ser in Wein ver-wan-delt.
marriage in Ga-li-lae - a, He hath chan-gèd some wa - ter in-to wine.
Er heil-te zwei Aus - - - sät-zi-ge von Ca -
He heal-èd two le - - - pers of Ca -
2nd Nazarene.
2. Nazarener.
211
Durch blo - sses Be - rüh-ren!
And He but touched them!
per - - na-um. Er hat auch Blin-de ge-heilt.
per - - na-um. He al-so heal-èd some blind men.
più espr.
espr.
Herodias.
O-ho!
Ho! ho!
Man hat ihn auf ei-nem Ber-ge im Ge-spräch mit En-geln ge-sehn!
Some have seen him on a mountain lis-te-ning to an-gels' talk.
espr.

A. 5503 F.

Herodias.
Ich glau-be nicht an Wun-der, ich ha-be ih-rer zu-vie-le ge-sehn!
Such mi-ra-cles are falsehood; in mi-ra-cles one should ne-ver be-lieve!
1 Naz.
Die Toch-ter des Ja-i-rus
The daugh-ter of Ja-i-rus
molto
mf
p
Herod (frightened)
Herodes (erschreckt).
212
Wie, er er-weckt die To-ten?
How! e'en the dead he rai-ses?
2nd Nazarene.
2. Nazarener.
Ja-
Yea,
1. Naz.
hat er von den To-ten er-weckt
He has rais-èd from the dead.
Ja-
Yea,
espr.
poco a poco più mosso
allmählich bewegter.
Herodes.
Ich ver-bie-te ihm, das zu tun.
I for-bid him to do such thing.
2. Naz.
wohl. Er er-weckt die To-ten.
Sire, He rais-èth the dead.
1. Naz.
wohl. Er er-weckt die To-ten.
Sire, He rais-èth the dead.
allmählich bewegter.
dim.
mf molto espr.

Herodes.
Es wä-re schrecklich, wenn die To-ten wie - der-kä-men! Wo ist der Mann zur
It would be dread-ful if to life the dead came a-gain! Where is this man at
getragen
mf
Zeit? 1st Nazarene.
present? 1. Nazarener.
Herr, er ist ü - ber- - all, a-ber es ist schwer, ihn zu
Sire, he is ev'-ry - where, but it's ve-ry hard, Sire, to
molto espr.
espr.
Der Mann muss ge-fun - den wer - den.
This Man must at once be found.
2. Nazarener.
2nd Nazarene. Es heisst, in Sa - ma-
They say, in Sa - ma-
1. Naz.
fin - den.
find him.
dim.
p

213
2. Naz.
ri - a wei - le er jetzt.
ri - a He may be found.
1. Naz.
Vor ein paar Ta - gen ver - liess er Sa - ma -
espr. But He hath left Sa - ma - ri - a since a
ri - a, ich glau - be, im Au - gen - blick ist er in der
few days a - go, and I think that by now He's in the
cresc.
214
Herod.
Herodes.
So hört: ich ver - bie - te ihm, die
Hear thou: I for - bid that by him the
Nä - he von Je - ru - sa - lem.
neighbourhood of Je - ru - sa - lem.
f
Herodes.
To - ten zu er - wecken!
dead should be a - wakened!
Es müsste schrecklich sein.
It would be ter - ri - ble.
Stimme des Jochanaan.
The Voice of Jokanaan.
O ü - ber die - ses gei - le Weib, die Toch - ter
Ah! the wan - ton! The har - lot! The daugh - ter of
pp
fp

215
Herodias (furiously) (wütend)
Be- Com-
Herodes.
wenn die To-ten wie - der-kä-men!
if to life the dead came a-gain!
Joch. Jok.
Ba - by-lons. So spricht der Herr, un-ser Gott:
Ba - by-lon. Thus saith the Lord, our God:
acceler.
mf
Ped
Più lento.
Langsamer. M. 𝅗𝅥=112
Herodias.
fiehl ihm, er soll schwei - gen.
mand him to be si - lent.
Ei-ne Menge Men - schen wird sich
There shall come up a mul-ti-
f
ff
p
pp
gegen sie sam-meln, und sie wer-den Stei - ne neh-men und sie stei - - -
tude of men against her, and they shall take stones and stone her, aye, and stone
cresc.

216
Herodias.
Joch. Jok.
Wahr - haf-tig, es ist schänd - lich!
You hear that! This is in - famous.
- ni-gen!
her to death!
Die Kriegshaupt - leu - te
The cap - tains_
ff
pp
wer-den sie mit ih-ren Schwertern durchboh - ren,
of the hosts with their sharp swords_ shall pierce her,
sie werden sie mit ih - ren
and with_ their hea - vy
p
217
Herodias.
Er soll schwei-gen, er soll
This is in - famous, this is
Schil - den zer - mal - - - - - men!
shields they will crush her!
pp
ff
schwei - gen!
in - fa - mous!
(broad)
(breit)
Es ist so, dass ich al - le Ver - rucht - heit
And thus it is that I'll wipe out all wi - ckedness
p
fz

218
Joch.
Jok.
aus - til - gen wer - de,
— from — the earth,
dass ich al - le Wei - ber leh - - -
and that all the wo - men shall
mf
f pp
- ren wer - de,
— now learn
nicht
not
auf den Wo - gen ih - rer Greu - el zu
to — i - mi - tate her a - bo - mi -
pp
sfz
pp
p
219
Herodias.
accel.er.
Du hörst,
You hear
was er ge - gen mich sagt, du
what he says a - gainst me? You al -
wan - deln!
na - tions!
mf sfz
f
sfz
Herodias
dul - dest es,
low him,
dass er die schmä - he, die dein Weib ist.
you al - low him to re - vile your wife?
Herodes.
Herod.
Er hat deinen Na -
He did not speak
f
sfz

meno mosso
wieder ruhiger
220 M. 𝅗𝅥 = 60
Herodes.
men nicht ge-nannt.
of you at all.
Stimme des Jochanaan
The Voice of Jokanaan.
(sehr feierlich) Es kommt ein Tag, da wird die
(very solemnly) There comes a day, then shall the
wieder ruhiger
M. 𝅗𝅥 = 60
pp una corda
Joch.
Jok.
Son - ne fin - ster wer - den wie ein schwarzes Tuch. Und der
sun turn black like sack - cloth of hair, and the
Mond wird wer - den wie Blut, und die Ster - ne des Him - mels wer - den zur
moon shall be - come like blood, and the stars of the hea - vens shall fall u -
221
Er - de fal - len wie un - rei - fe Fei - gen vom Fei - gen - baum.
pon the earth a - like ripe figs from the fig - tree.
A. 5503 F.

Joch.
Jok.
Es kommt ein Tag, wo die Kön'-ge der
There comes a day when the kings of the
senza cresc.
un poco più vivo
Etwas lebhafter.
222 Herodias.
Ha ha! Die-ser Prophet
Ah! Ah! This mad prophet
Er-de er-zit-tern.
earth shall be a-fraid!
Etwas lebhafter.
f tre corde
Herodias.
schwatzt wie ein Be-trun-ke-ner...
talks jus' like a drun-ken man...
A-ber ich kann den Klang
but I can-not suf-
stacc.
223 acceler.
sei-ner Stimme nicht er-tra-gen, ich has-se sei-ne Stimme.
-fer the sound of his voice, I hate this voice I'm hearing.
acceler.
cresc.

Herodias.
Be - fiehl ihm, er soll schwei - gen.
Com - mand him to be si - lent.

poco più tranquillo che prima

Herodes.
Herod.
p
Tanz für mich,
Dance for me,

etwas ruhiger als vorher M.M. 𝅗𝅥. = 60

ff **p**

Salome (ruhig) *(quietly)*
Ich ha - be kei - ne
I have no de -

Herodias. (heftig) *(with vehemence)*
Ich will nicht ha - ben, dass sie tanzt.
I will not have her danc - ing.

Herodes.
Sa - - - - - lo - me.
Sa - - - - - lo - mé.

224

Sal.
Lust, zu tan - zen, Te - trarch.
sire to dance. my lord.

Herodes.
Sa - - lo - me, Toch - ter der He -
Sa - - lo - mé, daugh - ter of He -

p **mf**

A. 5503 F.

123
225
Sal.
Ich will nicht tanzen, Te-
I care not, Te-trarch, to
Herodes
rodias, tanz für mich!
rodias, dance for me!
mf
f
Sal.
trarch
dance.
Herodias.
Du siehst, wie sie dir gehorcht.
You see how she obeys you.
Herodes
Salome, Salome, tanz für mich, ich
Salomé, Salomé, dance for me, I
Voice of Jokanaan.
Stimme des Jochanaan.
Er wird auf seinem Throne sitzen, er wird ge-
Upon his throne he shall be seated, he shall be
f
dim.
226
Herodes
bitte dich. Ich bin traurig heute Nacht, drum tanz für mich
beg of thee. I am very sad tonight, therefore dance for me,
Joch. Jok.
kleidet sein in Scharlach und Purpur.
clothèd in scarlet and purple.
dim.
mf
A. 5503 F.

Herodes.
Sa - lo-me, tanz für mich! Wenn du für mich
Sa - lo-me, dance for me! If you dance
Joch. Jok.
Und der En - gel des Herrn wird ihn dar-nie - der schla - gen.
And the an - gel of the Lord shall smite him.
più f
Herodes.
(pressingly)
(drängend)
tan - zest, kannst du von mir be - geh - ren, was du willst.
for me I'll al - low thee to ask of me what thou wilt.
Joch. Jok.
Er wird von den Wür - mern ge -
And the worms shall be
227
Herodes.
Ich wer - de es dir ge -
All you ask for I'll give
Joch. Jok.
fres - sen wer - den.
feed - ing on him.
mf cresc.
mf
f

A. 5503 F.

Salome (rising) (aufstehend)
Willst du mir wirk-lich
Will you indeed give me
Herodes.
ben.
thee.
Più tranquillo
Etwas ruhiger.
p dim.
pp
Sal
al-les ge-ben, was ich von dir be-geh-re,
what-so-e-ver I shall ask,
Tetrarch?
Tetrarch?
Herodias.
Tanze
Do not
mf
228
Herodias.
nicht, meine Toch-ter.
dance, my dear daughter.
Herodes.
Herod.
accelerando
Al-les, al-les, was du von mir be-geh-ren wirst;
All, all, what-so-e'er thou shalt ask of me,
f
fz

A 5503 F

Salome.

Du
You

Herodes.

rit.

und wärs die Hälf - te mei - nes Kö - nig - - reichs.
e'en to the half of my whole king - - - dom.

cresc.

Tempo primo
Früheres Zeitmass.

229

Sal.

schwörst es. Te - trarch?
swear it, Te - trarch?

Wo -
By

Herodes.

Ich schwör' es, Sa - lo - me.
I swear it, Sa - lo - me.

Früheres Zeitmass.

pp

sfz

dim.

Sal.

bei willst du das be - schwö - ren, Te - trarch?
what will you swear it, Te - trarch?

Herodes.

accelerando

Bei mei - nem Le - ben, bei mei - ner
By my life and by my

pp

fp

Herodias.
230
Tan-ze nicht, mei-ne Toch-ter!
Do not dance, my daughter!
Herodes.
Kro-ne, bei mei-nen Göt- - -tern. O Sa- - - - lo-me,
crown, and by my gods. O Sa - - - lo mé,
fp
p
p
tr
Salomé.
molto vivo
bereits ziemlich lebhaft
Du hast ei-nen
Re-mem-ber the
Herodes.
Sa- lo-me, tanz für mich!
Sa - lo-mé, dance for me!
cresc.
f
tr
dim. molto
Sal.
Eid geschwo-ren, Tetrarch.
oath you've ta-ken, Tetrarch.
231
Herodias.
Mei-ne
My
Herodes.
Ich ha-be ei-nen Eid geschwo-ren.
I'll ad-here to the oath I've ta-ken.
tr
pp
f

Herodias.
Toch-ter, tan-ze nicht.
daugh-ter, do not dance.
Herod.
Herodes. breit
Und wär's die Hälf-te mei-nes
E'en to the half of my whole
p
sffz
mf
Allegro molto
Sehr bewegt. M. 𝅗𝅥 = 76
Herodes
Kö-nigreichs.
king-dom.
232
Du wirst schön sein als
Thou'lt be fair as a
Timbales
f
p subito
233
(shivering)
erschauernd
Kö-ni-gin, un-er-mess-lich schön. Ah!
queen, will she not be fair? Ah!
p
es ist kalt hier. Es weht ein
it is cold here! There is an
pp
A. 5503 F.

Herodes.
eis - - - ger Wind, und ich hö - - - re.... wa - rum
i - - - cy wind, and I hear.......... where-fore
fpp
234
hö - - - re ich in der Luft die - ses Rau - - schen von
do I hear in the air all this beat - - ing of
marc.
Flü - - geln? Ah! Es ist doch so, als ob ein un - ge - heu -
great wings? Ah! Ah one might fan-cy 'twere a bird, a huge
cresc.
pp
- rer schwar - zer Vo - - - gel ü - ber der Ter - - ras - se schweb - te?
black bird in the air that ho - vers o'er the ter - race.
235
senza cresc.
p
espr.

Hero-des.
Wa-rum kann ich ihn nicht sehn, die-sen Vo - gel?
Ah! why can I not see it, where's this bird?
cresc.
fp
Die - ses Rau - - - schen ist schreck-lich. Es ist ein
But this beat - - - - ing is ter-rible. It is a
236
cresc.
fp
schnei - den - der Wind. A - ber nein, er ist nicht kalt, _
chill _ wind. Nay, 'tis not, it is not cold, _
marc.
mf
f
ff
237
_ er ist heiss. Giesst mir Was-ser ü-ber die Hän-de,
_ it is hot. Pour wa-ter o-ver my hands.
f
Ped.
f
*

238
Herodes.
gebt mir Schnee zu es-sen, macht mir den Man-tel los. Schnell,
Give me snow. I'm chok-ing. Loos-en my mant-le, quick. Quick,
(Viertel stets gleich)
sfz
239
schnell, macht mir den Mantel los! Doch nein! Lasst ihn! Die-ser
quick, loos-en my mantle, quick! But nay, leave it. It's my
ff sfz
mf
Kranz drückt mich. Die-se Ro-sen sind wie
gar-land that hurts me. Ah! these ro-ses are like
sempre accelerando
p
cresc.
240
(He tears the wreath from his head and throws it on the table.)
(Er reisst sich das Kranzgewinde ab und wirft es auf den Tisch.)
Feu-er.
fire.
Sehr schnell.
Presto
ff

A. 5503 F.

241
Herodes.
Ah! Jetzt kann ich at - men.
Ah! I can breathe now.
dim.
p
pp
mf
dim.
Jetzt bin ich glück - lich.
Now I am hap - py.
p
242 calando poco a poco
allmählich etwas ruhiger werdend
mf
poco f
espr.
p
dim.
Salomé.
Ich
I'll
Herodias.
Ich will nicht ha-ben, dass sie
I will not have it that she
(faintly)
(matt)
Herodes.
Willst du für mich tan-zen, Sa - lo - me?
Wilt thou not dance for me, Sa - lo - me?
pp
mf

(Sklavinnen bringen Salben und die sieben Schleier und nehmen Salome die Sandalen ab.)
(Slaves bring perfumes and the seven veils and take off Salome's sandals.)
Sal.
will für dich tan - zen.
dance for you, Te - trarch.
Herodias.
tan-ze!
dances!
Stimme des Jochanaan. The Voice of Jokanaan.
Wer ist Der, der von E - dom kommt,
Who is this who from E - dom com - eth,
243
(scoltamente)
(sehr fliessend) M. 𝅗𝅥 69
fp
pp
col Ped.
St. d. Joch.
wer ist Der, der von Bos - ra kommt, des - sen
who is this who from Boz - ra com - eth, and whose
Herodias.
Wir wol - len hin - ein - - - gehn.
Let us go with - - - in.
Kleid mit Pur - - - pur ge - färbt ist,
rai - - - ment is dy - - - èd with purp - le,
sempre pp
(more fiercely)
(immer heftiger)
Die Stim - me die - ses Menschen macht mich wahn - sinnig.
Let us go with - in, the voice of that man mad - dens me.
der in der Schön - heit sei - ner Ge - wän - der leuch -
who in the beau - - - ty of his gar - ments shin -
A. 5503 F.

Hero-dias.

Ich will nicht ha - ben, dass mei - ne

I will not have my

St. d. Joch.

- - - - - - - tet, der

- - - - - - - *èth? who*

244

Hero-dias.

Toch - ter tanzt, wäh - rend er im - mer da -

daugh - ter dance while he is con - tin - u - al-ly

St. d. Joch.

mäch - - - - - - - - tig in sei - ner

migh - - - - - - - - ty in His

pp

Hero-dias.

zwi - schen schreit.

cry - ing out.

St. d. Joch.

Grö - - - - - - - - sse wan - - - - - - -

great - - - - - - - - ness walk - - - - - - -

245
Herodias.
Ich will nicht ha-ben, dass sie tanzt, während du sie auf sol-che Art
I will not have her dance while you look at her in such a
St.d. Joch.
- - - delt, wa-rum ist dein Kleid mit
- - - eth? Where-fore is thy rai - - - - ment
sp
Herodias.
an - sichst. Mit einem Wort: ich will nicht ha - ben, dass sie tanzt.
fash - ion. In a word, I will not have my daughter dance.
Herod.
Herodes.
Steh nicht
Do not
St.d. Joch.
Schar - lach gefleckt?
stain - èd with scar - - - let?
accelerando
cresc.
f
Più mosso
Schneller.
Herodes.
auf, mein Weib, mei-ne Kö - nigin. Es wird dir nichts hel - fen,
rise, my wife, my queen, it will a - vail thee noth - ing.
f
p
sfz

Herodes.

ich ge - he nicht hin - ein, be - vor sie ge - tanzt hat.
I will not go with - in till she hath dan - cèd.

mf *sfz*

246

Herodes.

Tan - - ze Sa - - - lo - me, tanz für mich!
Dance, Sa - - - lo - mé, dance for me!

f

Herodias. 247

Tan - ze nicht, mei - ne Toch - ter!
Do not dance, my dear daugh - ter!

cresc.

Salomé.

Ich bin be - reit, Tetrarch.
I'm rea - dy now, my lord.

ff *mf (non arpeggiato)*

A. 5503 F.

 A. 5503 5507 5530 5534 F. Berlin, Adolph Fürstner.

*) stets mit den Niederstreich beginnen; niemals als Auftakt behandeln!
*) begin always with the down beat.
A 5508 5507 5530 5534 F.

A. 5503 5507 5530 5534 F.

A. 5503 5507 5520 5534 F.

cresc.
Vivace
Etwas lebhafter.
appassionato
molto dim.
ff
nuovamente tran-
wieder ruhiger
N
sfz dim.
p
quillo
grazioso
O
molto espr.
mf
f
p
pp

142
Vivace
etwas lebhafter
P
ff
sf
pp
calando
Primo tempo (abbastanza moderato)
wieder erstes Zeitmass.
(ziemlich langsam)
espr.
p
col Ped.
Q
col Ped. sempre
più espr.
allmählich etwas fliessender
gradatamente ravvivando
mf
(Ped. mit jedem Takt!)
(Ped. with each bar)
A. 5503 5507 5530 5534 F.

R
f
cresc.
f
cresc.
ritard.
accelerando
dim.
pp
Viel bewegter. M. 𝅗𝅥 = 126
molto mosso
pp
S
sempre pp
p

A. 5503 5507 5530 5534 P.

W
nuovamente moderato
più f
poco accelerando
gradatamente ravvivando
allmählich bewegter
dim.
p
X
marc.
(Salome seems to faint for a moment.
(Salome scheint einen Augenblick zu ermatten,
f
dim.
now she pulls herself together like with new strength.)
jetzt rafft sie sich wie neubeschwingt auf.)
grazioso
accelerando
sfz
Molto presto
Y Sehr schnell. M. 𝅗𝅥 = 168
A. 5503 5507 5530 5534 F.

146
stacc.
pp
Z
p
a
stacc.
pp
b
marc.
Ped.
c
cresc.
f
col Ped. sempre
(wild)
d
f
mf
A. 5503 5507 5580 5634 F.

147
e
accelerando
f marc.
f
fff
g
ff marcatissimo
ff
h
ff
sempre più acceler.
fff
Ped.
A. 5503 5507 5530 5534 F.

Sehr schnell. Molto presto
ff
i
k
a tempo
Etwas langsamer.
(Salomé remains for an instant in a visionary attitude near the cis-
(Salome verweilt einen Augenblick in visionärer Haltung an der Ci-
dim.
pp
f
tern where Jokanaan is kept prisoner, -
sterne, in der Jochanaan gefangen gehalten wird, -
p
Sehr schnell. Molto presto
dann stürzt sie vor und
then she throws herself at
zu Herodes Füssen.)
Herod's feet.)

Molto vivo
Sehr lebhaft.
Herod.
Ah! Herr - lich! Wun - - der-voll, wun -
Ah! won - drous! Won - - der-ful, won -
ff
f
p
mf
- der-voll! Siehst du, sie hat für mich ge-tanzt,
- der-ful! Ah! you see, she has danced for me,
(zu Herodias)
(to Herodias)
248
dei-ne Toch - ter. Komm her, Sa - lo-me, komm her, du sollst dei-nen
your fair daugh - ter. Come near, Sa - lo-me, come near, that to thee thy re -
espr.
dim.
Lohn ha-ben. Ich will dich kö-niglich be-loh - nen. Ich will dir
ward be giv'n. I'll pay thee roy-al-ly, my prin - cess. I'll give thee
249
cresc.

A. 5503 F.

Herodes.
al-les ge - - ben, was dein Herz begehrt. Was willst du
what-so-e - - ver thy soul de-si-reth. What wouldst thou
Lento
doppelt so langsam ♩ = 𝅗𝅥 des vorigen Zeitmasses.
Salome (süss) p (sweetly)
Ich möchte, dass sie mir gleich in ei-ner
I would that they presently bring me in a
ha - ben? Sprich!
have? Speak!
doppelt so langsam ♩ = 𝅗𝅥 des vorigen Zeitmasses.
dim. molto
250 Doppio movimento
Wieder doppelt so schnell.
Sal.
Sil - berschüssel....
sil - ver charger....
In ei-ner Sil - berschüssel gewiss doch in ei-ner
In a sil - ver charger sure - ly, in a
Wieder doppelt so schnell.
Sil - ber-schüssel....
sil - ver char-ger....
Sie ist rei - zend, nicht?
She is char - ming, aye?

Herodes.
Was ist's, das du in ei-ner Sil - - ber-schüs-sel ha - ben möch-test,
What is't thou wouldst have in a sil - - ver char - gen say, what is it,
251
o sü - sse, schö - ne Sa - - lo - me, du, die schöner ist, - als
O sweet and fai - rest Sa - - lo - mé, who art fair - er — than
sfz
al - - le Töch - ter Ju - dä - - as?
all the daugh - ters of Ju - dæ - - a?
Was sol - len sie
What wouldst thou have them
p
252
dir in ei - ner Sil - ber-schüs-sel brin - gen?
bring thee in a sil - ver char - ger, tell me?

253
Hero-des.
Sag es mir!
Tell me now!
Was es auch sein mag,
What-e-ver't may be.
sfz
accelerando
du sollst es er-hal-ten. Meine Reich-tü-mer
to thee 't will be gi-ven. All my trea-sures, they
p
254 Lento
doppelt so langsam.
dim.
ge-hö-ren dir.
be-long to thee.
Was ist es, das du ha-ben möchtest,
What is it that thou wouldst de-sire,
tr
f
sfz molto dim.
(Salomé rises.)
(Salome steht auf)
Salomé. (smiling)
(lächelnd)
pp
Den Kopf des Jo-cha-na-an.
The head of Jo-ka-na-an.
Sa-lome?
Sa-lomé?
ritard.
a tempo
pp

A. 5503 F.

Allegro
Schnell. M. 𝅗𝅥 = 72
Herodias.
Ah! das sagst du
Ah! that thou say'st
(rising abruptly)
(fährt auf)
Herodes.
Nein, nein!
No, no!
Schnell.
ff
Herodias.
gut, mei-ne Toch-ter. Das sagst du
well, my dear daugh-ter, that thou say'st
Herodes.
Nein, nein, Sa-lo-me;
No, no, Sa-lo-mé;
das ist es nicht,
thou dost not ask
f
255
Herodias.
gut!
well!
Herodes.
was du begehrst!
that of me!
Hör nicht auf die Stimme dei-ner Mutter. Sie gab dir
Do not lis-ten to the voice of your mother. She's e-ver
p
fp
f

A. 5503 F.

lento
doppelt so langsam.
Salome.
Ich ach-te
I do not
Herodes.
im-mer schlech - - ten Rat.
giving e - - vil coun-sel.
Ach - te nicht auf sie.
Do not heed her words.
cresc.
fp
Sal.
nicht auf die Stimme meiner Mut-ter.
heed the voice of my mo-ther.
256
Zu meiner eig - nen Lust will ich den
'Tis for mine own pleasure that I ask the
pp
cresc.
p
Kopf des Jo-cha-na-an in ei-ner Sil-berschüssel ha-ben.
head of Jo-ka-na-an in a sil-ver charger, Te-trarch.
Du hast ei-nen
Re-member the
Eid geschworen, He-ro-des. Du hast ei-nen
oath you've ta-ken, He-rod. Re-mem-ber the
257
Eid geschworen, ver-
oath you've ta-ken, re-
cresc.

accelerando

Presto

Sehr schnell. M 𝅗𝅥. = 88

Sal.

giss das nicht!
member well!

Herodes. (hastig) (*hastily*)

Herod. Ich weiss, ich ha - be ei - nen Eid ge - schwo - ren. Ich weiss es
I know, I know the oath I've ta - ken, I know it

Sehr schnell.

f

sfz

Herodes. wohl. Bei mei - nen Göt - tern ha - be ich ge - schworen. A - ber ich be - schwöre dich,
well. Yes, I have sworn an oath, I know it. But I pray thee,

258

mf

dim.

p

Herodes. Sa - lo - me, ver - lan - ge et - was and' - res von mir. Ver -
Sa - lo - me, ask of me some - thing else. Ask

f

dim.

259

Herodes. lan - ge die Hälf - te meines Kö - nig - reichs. Ich will sie dir
of me the half of my whole king - dom, and I will

(drängend)

p

p

cresc.

260
Herodes.
ge - ben. A-ber ver - lan - - - ge nicht von mir, was deine Lip - pen ver -
give it thee. But do not ask of me what thy lips have just
Lento
langsam ♩=𝅗𝅥 des vorigen Zeitmasses.
Salomo. (stark) (powerfully)
261
Ich ver-lan-ge von dir den Kopf des Jo - chan-na-an.
I ask of you the head of Jo ka - na-an.
Herodes.
lang-ten.
ask - ed.
Nein nein, ich will ihn dir nicht
No, no, I do not wish to
langsam ♩=𝅗𝅥 des vorigen Zeitmasses.
Molto allegro
Sehr schnell. M. 𝅗𝅥. = 72
Sal.
Du hast ei-nen Eid geschworen. He - - ro - - - des.
You have sworn an oath, re-mem-ber, He - - - - - rod.
Herodias.
Ja, du hast ei - - nen
Yes, you have sworn an
Herodes.
ge - ben.
give it.
Sehr schnell.
cresc.

262

Herodias: Eid geschworen. Alle haben es gehört.
oath before all. Everybody heard you.

Herodes: Still,
Peace,

Herodes: Weib, zu dir spreche ich nicht.
woman! 'tis not to you I speak.

Herodias: Meine Tochter hat recht daran getan, den Kopf des Jochanaan zu verlangen. Er hat mich mit
It was well of my daughter to ask the head of Jokanaan, she is quite right. He has said

Herodias: Schimpf und Schande bedeckt. Man kann sehn, dass sie ihre
monstrous things against me. One can see that she loves her

263

f *mf* *p* *fp* *sfz*

Herodias.

Mutter liebt. Gib nicht nach, meine Tochter, gib nicht nach! Er
mother well. Do not yield my daughter, do not yield! He

p *f*

Ped. *

264

Herodias.

hat einen Eid geschworen.
has sworn an oath my daughter.

Herod. Herodes.

Still,
Peace!

ff *f* *ff*

più tranquillo
Etwas ruhiger

265

Herodes.

sprich nicht zu mir! Salome, ich beschwöre dich:
speak not to me! Salome, I beseech thee

dim. *p espress.*

Herodes.

Sei nicht trotzig! Sieh, ich habe dich
be not stubborn! Come, have I not

espress. *pp* *marc. espress. dolce* *pp*

266

Herodes.

— immer lieb — ge - habt. Kann sein, — ich
— e-ver lov - ed thee? Per - chance, — I have

espress. espress.

Herodes.

accelerando

ha - be dich — zu lieb ge - habt. Da-rum ver - lan-ge
lo - vèd thee — too much, my child. Therefore do not ask

espress.

più vivo
lebhafter 267

Herodes.

das nicht von mir. — Der
this thing of me. — The

pp

Herodes.

Kopf ei - nes Mannes, der vom Rumpf ge - trennt ist, ist ein
head of a dead man that is cut from its bo - dy is too

f p

268
Hero-des.
üb - ler An-blick. Hör, was ich sa-ge!
vile to look at. Hear what I tell you!
dim.
un poco meno mosso
ritard.
269 etwas ruhiger (wiegend) M. 𝅗𝅥. = 66.
Ich ha-be ei-nen Sma - ragd. Er ist der
I have an em - e - rald. It is the
p espr.
dim.
pp
schön - ste Sma-ragd der gan - zen Welt.
fin - est em' - rald in the whole world.
accelerando
Den willst du
Thou wilt take
270 Tempo primo.
ha-ben, nicht wahr? Ver-lang ihn von mir, ich
that, wilt thou not? Ask it of me, thou
espress.

A. 5503 F.

Herodes.
will ihn dir ge - ben, den schön - - - - sten Sma -
shallst at once have it, the fin - - - est em-
cresc.
dim.
Lento
langsam ♩ = 𝅗𝅥. des vorigen Zeitmasses
Salomé.
271
accelerando
Ich for - dre den Kopf des Jo - cha - na - an.
I ask for the head of Jo - ka - na - an.
Herodes.
ragd.
rald.
Du hörst nicht zu, du hörst nicht
Thou art not listening, thou art not
langsam ♩ = 𝅗𝅥. des vorigen Zeitmasses
p
espress.
sfz
Tempo primo.
Sal
Den Kopf des Jo -
The head of Jo -
Herodes.
zu. Lass mich zu dir reden, Sa - lo - me!
listening. Be rea - sonable, listen, Sa - lo - me!
Tempo primo.
sfz
272
Sal
cha - na - an.
ka - na - an.
Herodes.
Das sagst du nur, um mich zu quä - len, weil ich dich so an - geschaut habe. Deine
Thou say - est that to give me trouble, because I have looked at thee. Thy
fz
ff
dim.
A 5503 F.

doppio movimento
doppelt so schnell M. 𝅗𝅥 = 100
273
Herodes.
Schön - heit hat mich ver - wirrt.
beau - ty has be - reft me.
Oh! Oh!
Oh! Oh!
p cresc.
ff espress.
agitato
Bringt Wein! Mich dür - stet.
Bring wine! I'm thirs - ty.
dim. p
274
Sa - lo - me,
Sa - lo - mé,
espress.
p
pp
Sa - lo - me, lass uns wie Freun - de zu ein - an - der sein!
Sa - lo - mé, let us be friends. ah, come near to me!
espress.
Be - denk dich!
Be - think thee —
Ah!
Ah!
dim.
pp
A. 5503 F.

275
Herodes.
Was wollt ich sa - gen?
What would I tell thee?
Was war's?....
What was't?....
pespress.
Hero-des.
Ah!
Ah!
Ich weisses wie - der!...
I re - mem - ber!
Molto vivo
276 Sehr bewegt
Sa -
Sa -
p
pp espress.
Herodes.
lo - me,
lo - me,
du kennst
thou know -
mei - ne wei - ssen
- est my white
pp
Herodes.
Pfau - - - - en, meine
pea - - - - cocks, aye, my
schö - nen, wei - ssen Pfau - en, die im
beau - ti - ful white pea - cocks, that are

277
Herodes
Gar - ten zwi-schen den Myr - - ten wan - - - deln. Ich
walking in the gardens be - tween the myrt - - - les. I'll
pp
espr.
will sie dir al - le, al - le ge - ben. In der gan - zen
give them all, all of them I'll give thee. In the whole
espr.
cresc.
278
Welt lebt kein Kö - nig, der sol-che Pfau - - en hat. Ich ha-be blos hun - - -
world there's no king who has peacocks like un-to mine. I have but a hun - - -
f
mf subito
p
Lento
Salome. 279 Langsam des vorigen Zeitmasses.
Gib mir den
Give me the
- dert. A - ber al - le will ich dir ge - - - ben.
- dred. But I will give them all to thee.
cresc.
f

Molto allegro
Sehr schnell. M. 𝅗𝅥. = 72
Sal.
Kopf des Jo - cha - - na - an!
head of Jo - ka - - na - an!
Herodias.
Gut gesagt, mei - ne Toch - ter!
Well said, my dear daugh - ter!
Sehr schnell.
ff
(to Herod)
(zu Herodes)
280
Hero-dias.
Und du, du bist lä - cherlich mit dei - nen
But you, you're ri - di - cu - lous with all your
Herod.
Herodes.
Still, Weib! Du krei - schest wie ein Raub - vo - gel.
Si - lence! You cry out like a beast of prey.
Hero-dias.
Pfau - en.
pea - cocks.
Hero-des.
Dei - ne Stim - me pei - nigt mich. Still, sag ich dir!
Your voice doth wea - ry me. Si - lence, I say!
un poco ritard.
pp
f
p

281 Molto agitato
Sehr bewegt ♩ schneller als vorher ♩. M. ♩= 108
Herodes.
Sa-lo-me, be-denk, was du tun willst. Es kann sein,
Sa-lo-mē, just think what thou'rt do-ing. Peop-le say
f espress.
dim.
p
pespr.
282
dass der Mann von Gott ge-sandt ist.
of this man that God hath sent him.
(weich)
espress.
pp
283
accelerando
Er ist ein heil-ger Mann. Der Fin-ger
He is a ho-ly man. The fin-ger of
(sanft)
pp
p
espress.
cresc.
Got-tes hat ihn be-rührt. Du möchtest nicht,
God perchance has touch'd him. Thou wouldst not that
f molto appassionato

284
Herodes.
dass mich ein Un-heil trifft, Sa - lo - me? Hör jetzt auf mich!
some harm should happen to me? Sa - lo - mé? Lis - ten to me!
p
Lento
mehr als doppelt so langsam
doppio movimento
Sehr schnell. M. 𝅗𝅥 = 100
Salomé.
Ich will den Kopf des Jo - cha - na - an.
Give me the head of Jo - ka - na - an.
(bursting out)
(auffahrend)
Herodes.
Ah!
Ah!
mehr als doppelt so langsam
Sehr schnell.
ff
Herodes.
Du willst nicht auf mich hö - ren.
I see now, thou'lt not lis - ten.
ff
dim.
285
poco a poco calando
allmählich etwas beruhigen
Herodes.
Sei ruhig, Sa - lo - me.
Be calm, Sa - lo - mé!
f
A. 5503 F.

Herodes.
Ich — siehst du,
I. — look you,
286
accelerando
bin ru - hig. Hö - re:
am quite calm. Lis - ten:
espr.
p
Molto allegro
wieder äusserst schnell M. 𝅗𝅥 = 104.
(leise und heimlich) (low and secret)
Ich ha-be an die-sem Ort Ju-we-len ver-steckt, Ju-we-len, die selbst dei-ne
I have hid-den in this place some mar-vel-lous je-wels, je-wels that e-ven thy
pp
287
Mut-ter nie ge-se-hen hat. Ich ha-be ein Halsband mit vier — Rei-hen
mo-ther has ne-ver seen. I have a col-lar with four — rows of
poco marcato
p

288
Herodes.
Per - - - len, To-pa - se, gelb wie die Au-gen der Ti - ger. To-
pearls. To-pa - zes, yellow like the eyes of a ti - ger. To-
fp
p espr.
Herodes.
pa - se, hell - rot, wie die Au - gen der Wald - tau - be,
pa - zes, quite pink, as the eyes of the wood - pi - - geon,
espr.
Herodes.
und grü - ne To - pa - se, wie Katzen-au - gen. Ich ha - be O -
and green_ to - pa - zes, like Persian cats' eyes. And I have
dim.
espr.
pp
289
Herodes.
pa - le, die immer fun - keln, mit ei - nem Feu - er, kalt wie Eis.
o - pals that burn al - ways, with a flame as cold as ice.
cresc.
fp

290
accelerando
Herodes.
Ich will sie dir al - le ge - ben, al - le.
I will give them all to thee, all, all.
mf
cresc.
(with still more agitation)
(immer aufgeregter)
äusserst bewegt und stets drängend
molto agitato
Ich ha - be Chryso - li - the und Be - ryl - le, Chryso - pra - se und Ru -
I have some chryso - lit - es and be - ryls, chry - so - pa - ses and dark
M. ♩ = 112.
f
espr.
p
291
bi - ne. Ich ha - be Sar - do - nyx und Hy - a - cinth stei - ne und Stei - ne von Chal -
ru - bies. I have some sar - do - nyx and hy - a - cinth stones, al - so stones of chal - ce -
f
dim.
ce - don. Ich will sie dir al - le ge - ben, al - le und noch an - dre Din - ge.
do - ny, and I will give them all un - to thee, and o - ther things shall be ad - ded.
p
mf
p
f
292
Ich ha - be ei - nen Kristall, in den zu schaun keinem Wei - be ver -
I have a mar - vel - lous crys - tal in - to which to look 'tis not law - ful for
ff
pp
A. 5503 F.

293
Herodes.
gönnt ist. In ei-nem Per-len-mut-ter-käst-chen ha-be ich drei wun-der-ba-re Tür-
wo-men. In a small box of nacre I'm hol-ding three lit-tle won-der-ful tor-
pp
ki-se: wer sie an sei-ner Stir-ne trägt, kann Din-ge sehn,
quoi-ses. Who wears them on his fore-head can i-ma-gine things
espr.
mf
294
die nicht wirklich sind. Es sind un-be-zahl-ba-re Schät-ze.
which are ne-ver real. These are trea-sures be-yond all trea-sures.
dim.
pp
f
dim.
sempre più agitato
Was be-gehrst du sonst noch, Sa-lo-me? Al-les,
What be-sides de-si-rest thou, Sa-lo-me? Ah! what-
pp
mf
dim.
295
was du ver-langst, will ich dir ge-ben, nur ei-nes
e-ver thou ask'st I'll glad-ly give thee, all, save one

sempre stringendo
immer schneller
Herodes.
nicht: Nur nicht das
thing. I'll give thee
molto cresc.
296
Le-ben die-ses ei - nen Man - nes.
all things save the life of this man
cresc.
297
Ich will dir den Man - tel des Ho - hen-priesters
I will give thee e - ven the man - tle of the
ge - ben. Ich will dir den Vor - hang
High Priest. I'll give thee the veil, hear
A. 5503 F.

173
(broad)
(breit)
(The Jews: oh! oh! oh!)
(Die Juden: Oh Oh Oh!)
Herodes.
— des Al - ler - hei - - - - lig - sten ge - ben....
— me, of the ho - - - - ly — shrine. —
Lento
Langsam. (ferociously)
Salome (wild)
Gib mir den Kopf des Jo - cha - - - na - an!
Give me the head of Jo - ka - - - na - an!
dim.
298 (Herod, in despair —, sinks back in his seat.)
(Herodes sinkt verzweifelt auf seinen Sitz zurück.)
Allegro
Sehr schnell. M. 𝅗𝅥 = 72.
Herod (faintly)
Herodes (matt)
Man soll ihr ge-ben, was sie ver-langt!
Let her be gi-ven what she — asks!
299
Sie ist in
She is in -
A. 5503 F.

174
Herodes.
ritard.
Allegro
bewegt M. 𝅗𝅥 = 72.
Wahr - - - - - - Heit
deed, ah,
ihrer Mutter Kind.
her mother's child!
pp
ff
(Herodias draws from the hand of the Tetrarch the ring of death and gives it to the first soldier, who straightway bears
(Herodias zieht dem Tetrarchen den Todesring vom Finger und gibt ihn dem ersten Soldaten, der ihn auf der Stelle dem
300
sfz
ff
p
ff
it to the Executioner.)
Henker überbringt.)
301
mf
ff
Herod.
Herodes.
Wer hat mei-nen Ring ge-nommen?
Who has ta-ken my ring from me?
p
p
cresc.
A. 5503 F.

(The Executioner goes down into the cistern.)
(Der Henker geht in die Cisterne hinab.)
302
marcatissimo
Herod.
Herodes.
Ich hat-te ei-nen Ring an mei-ner rech-ten Hand.
I surely had a ring just now on my right hand.
Wer hat meinen Wein ge-trunken? Es war
Who has drain'd my goblet of wine? There was
Wein in meinem Be-cher. Er war mit Wein gefüllt. Es hat ihn jemand
wine in my gob-let. It was still full of wine. Some-bo-dy has been
303
aus-ge-trun-ken.
drinking of it.
(low)
(leise)
Oh! gewiss wird Un-heil
Oh! I'm sure, mis-for-tune
pp (seufzend)
V. 5503 F.

Herodias. ff
Mei-ne Toch-ter hat recht getan!
My dear daughter has right - - - - - ly done!
Herodes.
ü-ber ei-nen kommen.
will be-fall some of us.
304
Ich bin si-cher, es wird ein Un-heil ge-
I am cer-tain that some mis-for-tune will
schehn.
come.
(Salomé leans over the cistern and listens.)
(Salome an der Cisterne lauschend.)
immer äusserst bewegt.
molto cresc.
sempre molto mosso
305 Salomé.
Es ist kein Laut zu ver-neh-men. Ich
There is no sound. I hear no-thing. There's

Sal.
hö - re nichts.
not a sound.
Wa-rum schreit er nicht, der Mann?
Wherefore cries he not, this man?
Ah! Wenn ei-ner mich zu tö - ten kä - me, ich wür-de
Ah! if a-ny man would come to kill me, ah, I would
cresc.
306
schrei-en, ich wür-de mich weh-ren, ich wür-de es nicht dul - - den!...
cry out, I would struggle, no, no, I would not bear it!
kurz
Schlag zu, schlag zu Na - a-man, schlag zu, sag' ich dir...
Now strike, now strike Na - a-man, now strike, I tell you...
ff
dim.
p
dim.

Sal.
Nein, ich hö-re nichts.
No, I hear no sound.
pp
sfz
molto agitato
(drawn)
(gedehnt) ritenuto
a tempo 307
äusserst bewegt.
Es ist ei-ne schreck-li-che Stil-le!
There is such a ter-ri-ble si-lence!
Ah! Es ist et-was zu
Ah! Some-thing has
ff
Bo-den ge-fal-len. Ich hör-te et-was fal-len.
fallen to the ground. I have heard something falling.
Es war das Schwert des Henkers.
It was the sword of the headsman.
sempre più vivo
308
Er hat Angst, die-ser Skla-ve.
He is frigh-tend, this heads-man.

Sal.

Er hat das Schwert fal - len las - sen! Er
He has let fall his sword! He

M. 𝅗𝅥 = 72

sfz *p* *pp*

309

Sal.

traut sich nicht, ihn zu tö - - ten. Er ist ei-ne Memme,
is a-fraid to be - head him. Oh! he is a coward,

p *cresc.*

310 *(to the page)*
(zum Pagen)

Sal.

die - ser Skla - ve. Schickt Sol - da - ten hin! Komm hierher, du
this weak heads - man. Send some sol-diers down! Come hither, thou

f

Sal.

warst der Freund die - ses To - - ten, nicht? Wohl - an, ich sa -
wert the friend of this dead man, aye? Look thou, I tell

dim. *p* *cresc.* *sfz*

311

Sal.

- ge dir: Es sind noch nicht ge-nug To - - - te. Geh zu den Sol-
thee, there are not yet e-nough dead men. Quick, go to the

dim. p cresc. sfz

da-ten und be-fiehl ih-nen, hin - ab - zu-stei-gen und mir zu
sol-diers, go and bid them des-cend to the cis-tern and bring the

molto cresc.

ho - len, was ich ver-lan-ge, was der Te-trarch mir ver-spro-chen hat, was
thing that I am as-king, the thing the Te - trarch has pro-mised, which is

sfz

312 sempre accelerando

mein ist! Hier-her, ihr Sol-da-ten, geht ihr in die Ci-
mine! Come hi-ther, ye sol-diers, go down in-to this

f sfz sfz

Sal.
ster- - ne hin - un - ter
cis - tern, get ye down,
und holt mir den Kopf des Man - - - nes!
and bring me the head of the pro - - - phet!
cresc.
313
(shouting)
(schreiend)
Te-tarch, Te - tarch, be - fiehl deinen Sol - da - ten, dass sie mir den
My lord, my lord, com - mand your soldiers that they bring me the
Kopf des Jocha - - - - - - naan ho - len!
head of Jo - ka - - - - - na - an, my lord!
(Ein riesengrosser, schwarzer Arm, der Arm des Henkers, streckt sich aus der Cisterne heraus, auf einem silbernen Schild den Kopf des Jochanaan haltend, Salome ergreift ihn.)
(A huge black arm of the executioner, comes forth from the cistern, bearing on a silver shield the head of Jokanaan Salomé seizes it.)
M. ♩ 72
Andante
Ziemlich langsam.
(Viertel)
ff
cresc.
p
cresc.
314
sfz
ff

182
Sal.
Ah! Du woll-test mich nicht deinen Mund küs- -sen lassen,
Ah! thou wouldst not suf - for me to kiss thy mouth, thou wouldst not,
p
Jocha- - na-an!
Jo-ka- - -na-an!
cresc.
315
Wohl,
Well,
ff
più lento
ritard.
Etwas breit.
ich werde ihn jetzt küs- - - sen.
well, it shall now be kiss- - - ed.
dim.
M. ♩. = 60
f
316
ff
A. 5503 F.

Sal.
Ich will mit meinen Zäh - nen hin-
And with my teeth I'll bite it I
accelr.
espr.
318
ein - beis - - - sen, wie man in ei - ne rei - - fe Frucht beis-
will bite it as one bites in a ripe fruit. I
dim.
p
espr.
cresc.
- sen mag.
said I would.
sfz
ritard.
319
Ja, ich will ihn jetzt
Yes I will kiss
più largo
noch breiter
molto espr.
p
pp
f molto dim.

A. 5503 F.

poco a poco più a tempo primo
wieder allmählich im Zeitmass.
320
Sal.
küs-sen, dei- - - - nen Mund, Jo-cha - na - an.
it now, kiss thy mouth, Jo-ka - na - an.
espr.
pp
Ich hab' es ge-sagt.
I said that I would.
espr.
p
espr.
321
Hab' ich's nicht gesagt?
Did I not say it?
Ja, ich hab' es ge-
Yes, yes, so I have
cresc.
sagt.
said.
Ah! Ah!
322
Ich will ihn jetzt
I will now kiss
f
ppp

etwas fliessender
un poco più mosso
M. ♩= 72
Sal.
küs - - - - - sen...
kiss thy mouth.
espr.
ppp
pp
323
A-ber wa-rum siehst du mich nicht an, Jo-cha - -
But where-fore dost thou not look at me Jo-ka - -
- na-an? Deine Au - - - gen, die so schreck - - lich wa-ren
- na-an? Thine eyes that were so ter - - - ri - ble,
324
so voller Wut und Verachtung, sind jetzt geschlossen. Warum sind sie ge-
so full of rage and contempt, they are now closed Wherefore then are they
smorzando
p
sfz
mf
pp
espr.
smorz.
A. 5503 5511 F.

ritard. a tempo

Sal.: schlossen? Öff-ne doch die Au-gen, so he-be dei-ne Li-der, Jo-cha-
clo-sèd? O-pen thou thine eyes, lift up a-gain thine eye-lids, Jo-ka-

pp — p marc. — pp

325

Sal.: -na-an! Wa-rum siehst du mich nicht an? Hast du
-na-an! Why dost thou not look at me? Art thou a-

molto espr. — f — dim. — Ped.

Sal.: Angst vor mir, Jo-cha-na-an, dass du mich nicht an-
fraid of me? Jo-ka-na-an that thou wilt not look

p espr. — cresc. — f — Ped.

calando 326 a tempo M. ♩= 72

Sal.: -se-hen willst? Und dei-ne Zun-ge, sie
at me? And thy red tongue doth

(kurz und hart)

dim — p — espr cantabile — p — pp

Sal.

sprichtkein Wort, Jo - cha - - na-an, die-se Scharlachnat-ter, die ih-ren
speak no word, (sotto) Jo - ka - - na-an, that scar-let vi-per spatting its

327

Gei - fer ge - gen mich spie. Es ist selt-sam, nicht?
poi - son, it stirs no more. It is stran-ge, aye?

cresc. *pp*

Wie kommt es, dass die-se ro-te Nat-ter sich
How is it that this small scarlet vi-per doth

cresc.

328

nicht mehr rührt? __
stir no more? __

dim. *p* *espr.*

A. 5503 5511 F.

Sal.

Du sprachst bö-se Wor - te ge-gen mich, ge-gen
Thou didst use e-vil lan-guage a-gainst me, a-gainst

cresc.

Sal.

mich, Sa - - lo-me, die Toch-ter der He-ro - di-as, Prin-zes - sin von Ju -
me, Sa - lo-mé, the daughter of He-ro - di-as, Prin-cess of Ju -

fp cresc. *fp* cresc.

marc

329 accelerando

più mosso

Ziemlich lebhaft.

Sal.

dä - - a. Nun wohl!
dae - - a. Well then!

M. ♩= 96

f *f*

Sal.

330

Ich le - be noch, a - ber du bist tot, und dein Kopf,
I'm li - ving still, but thou art dead, and thy head,

f *sf* *ff*

immer bewegter.
sempre più mosso
Sal.
dein Kopf ge-hört mir! Ich kann mit ihm tun, was ich will. Ich kann ihn den Hun - den vor - wer - fen und den Vö - geln der Luft. Was die Hun - - - - - - de üb - rig las-sen, sol-len die Vö - gel der Luft
thy head belongs to me! I'm free to do with it what I will. I may give it the dogs to feed on, and the birds in the air. What is left by the dogs may be de - voured by the birds
331
ff
p
f
sfz
mf
dim.
A. 5503 5511 F.

332
Sal.
ver - zeh - ren....
of the air.
cresc.
accelerando molto
Ah! Ah! Jo - cha - na -
Ah! Ah! Jo - ka - na -
p
molto cresc.
f
ff
poco ritardando.
an, Jo - cha - na - an, du warst
an, Jo - ka - na - an, thou wert
dim.
espr.
Un poco mosso
Zart bewegt.
333
schön.
fair!
M. 𝅗𝅥 = 52
Dein Leib war ei - ne El -
Thy bo - dy was a co -
p (sehr singend)
pp
pp
Ped. tenuto

191
334
Sal.
fen-bein-säu - le auf sil-ber-nen Füs - sen. Er war ein
lumn of i - vo-ry set on a sil - ver socket. It was a
pp
Gar - ten vol-ler Tau - ben in der Sil - ber-li - lien
gar - den full of do - ves. full of sil - ver li - lies'
cresc.
dim.
sempre più mosso 335
immer fliessender im Zeitmass.
molto appassionato
Glanz. Nichts in der Welt war so weiss wie dein
shine. No thing on earth was so white as thy
pp
cresc.
f espr.
dim.
Leib. Nichts in der Welt war so schwarz wie dein
skin. No thing on earth was so black as thy
p
f
fp
dim.
A 5503 5511 F.

336
Sal.
Haar. In der gan - zen Welt war nichts
hair. And in all the world was no -
pp
cresc.
espr.
f
tr
ritard.
337 Un poco più tranquillo (ma sempre alla breve)
Etwas ruhiger (aber stets ¢).
so rot wie dein Mund.
-thing so red as thy mouth.
M. 𝅗𝅥 = 44
pp
dim.
p
marc.
marc.
p
Dei - ne Stim - me war ein Wei -
But thy voice was a cen -
pp
pp
tr
338
accelerando
- rauch - ge - fäss und wenn ich dich
- ser of sweet scents, and when I looked
marc.
pp
marc.
tr
Ped.
*
A. 5503 5511 F.

lento (sempre ¢)
ritard. più ritard. langsam (stets ¢).
Sal.
an-sah, hör - te ich ge-heim - nis-vol-le Mu - sik...
on thee I could hear a mu - - - sic of strange sounds
dim. pp espr.
339
cresc. dim.
(Lost in thought as she gazes upon Jokanaan's head)
(In den Anblick von Jochanaans Haupt versunken.)
340
Ah! Wa-rum
Ah! Wherefore
l.H. pp mf espr.
ritard. a tempo
hast du mich nicht an - ge - sehn, Jo - cha -
didst thou ne - ver look at me, Jo - ka -
pp
allmählich fliessender.
poco accelerando
un poco più mosso
Etwas bewegter. M. ♩= 60.
na - an? Du leg - test ü-ber dei-ne Au - gen die
na - an? Thou didst put u-pon thine eyes the
p espr.
A. 5503 5511 F.

sempre più vivo
341 immer lebhafter.
Sal.
Bin - de ei - - nes, der sei - nen Gott schau - en woll -
cov'ring of him who seek - eth God in all His glo -
p espr.
- te. Wohl! Du hast dei-nen Gott ge-sehn, Jo-cha - - na-an,
- ry. Well! Thou may'st have seen thy God, Jo - ka - - na-an,
fp
pp
342 accelerando
a - ber mich, mich, mich
but me, me, me,
cresc.
f
sempre più mosso
immer bewegter.
hast du nie ge - sehn. Hät-test du
thou didst ne - ver see. If thou hadst
molto espr.
espr.
p
espr.

343

Sal.

mich ge-sehn, du hät - test mich ge - liebt!
looked at me, thou wouldst have loved

cresc. — f — *appassionato*

Sehr bewegt. M. 𝅗𝅥 = 80 — *Molto mosso*

Sal.

Ich dür - ste nach dei - ner
me. I'm thir - sting for all thy

ff — p

344

Sal.

Schön - heit. Ich hung - re nach dei - nem
beau - ty. I'm hun - gry for thy bo - - -

f — pp

Sal.

Leib. Nicht Wein noch Äp - fel kön - - nen mein Ver - lan - gen
dy. Neither wine nor app - les can ap - pease all my de -

cresc. — espr. — dim. — tr

stringendo
Mit grosser Steigerung
345
Sal.
stil - len...
sire
espr.
Was soll ich jetzt tun, Jo-cha-
What shall I do now, Jo-ka-
p
cresc.
p
- na-an?
- na-an?
Nicht die Flu - ten,
Not by floods
346
noch die gro - ssen
nor by the great
cresc.
Was - ser
wa - tèrs
kön - nen die-ses brün - - - sti-ge Be-
can e - ver the heat of my strong
cresc.
f
geh - ren lö - - - schen...
passion be quen - - - ched
molto allegro
347 sehr lebhaft
Oh!
Oh!
Wa-rum
Wherefore
ff

più accelerando

Sal. sahst du mich nicht an? Hät-test du
didst thou not look at me? If thou hadst

cresc. *ff* *sfz* *f*

348 *lento* mehr als doppelt so langsam.

Sal. mich an-ge-sehn du hät-test mich ge-liebt.
look-èd at me thou wouldst have lov-èd me.

M. ♩ 63

mf *cresc.* *ff* *p* *espr.*

Sal. Ich weiss es wohl, du hät-test mich ge-
I know it well, thou wouldst have lov-ed

cresc. *molto* *ff*

349 molto ritenuto

Sal. liebt. Und das Ge-heim-nis der Lie-
me, and the great mys-te-ry of love

dim. *p* *dim.* *pp*

350
Sal.
- - - be ist grö - - sser als das Ge - heim - nis des
is grea - - ter than the myste - ry
dim.
ppp
pp
Sal.
To - des...
of death...
mässig bewegt
moderato
M. 𝅗𝅥 = 80.
pp
ppp
Herod (with lowered voice to Herodias)
Herodes (leise zu Herodias.)
351
Sie ist ein Un-ge-heu-er, dei-ne Tochter. Ich sa-ge dir, sie ist ein
She is a hi-deous monster, thy daughter. I tell it thee, she's al-to-
pp
Herodias (stark.)
(powerful)
Meine Tochter hat recht ge-tan. Ich möch - te jetzt hierbleiben.
I approve of my daugh-ter's deed. And I will now stay here.
Herodes
Un-ge-heuer!
gether monstrous!
Ah!
Ah!
ff
dim.
ff fz
trem.
A. 5503 F.

Herodes.
Da spricht meines Bruders Weib.
There speaks my brother's wife.
dim.
p
(weaker)
(schwächer)
Komm, ich will nicht an diesem Or-te blei-ben.
Come, I will no longer stay in this place.
352
(vehemently)
(heftig)
Komm, sag ich dir!
Come, I tell thee!
ff
p
Si-cher, es wird
Sure-ly, something
Schreck-li-ches ge-schehn.
ter-ri-ble will happen.
Wir wol-len uns im Pa-last ver-ber-gen,
Let us hide ourselves in the pa-lace.
He-ro-di-as, ich fan-ge
He-ro-di-as, I am be-
mf
353
(der Mond verschwindet)
an zu er-zit-tern...
ginning to tremble...
(the moon disappears)
sf
f
mf

A. 5503 F.

200
doppelt so schnell. molto allegro (doppio movimente)
(auffahrend) (rising suddenly)
Herodes.
Man - nas - sah, Is - sa - char, O - zi - as, löscht die
Ma - nas - seh, I - sa - char, O - zi - as, put out the
Fa - ckeln aus. Ver - bergt den Mond, ver - bergt die Ster - - - ne!
tor - ches. Hide the moon, hide the stars
ff
marc.
(the stage becomes very dark)
es wird ganz dunkel)
Es wird Schreck - li - ches ge - schehn.
Something ter - ri - ble will come.
cresc.
ff
Lento
doppelt so langsam.
dim.
pp
poco f
355
Salome (faintly) (matt) sehr gedehnt M. ♩=58.
Ah! Ich ha - be dei - nen Mund ge - küsst. Jo - cha -
Ah! I have kissed thy mouth. Jo - ka -
A.5503 F.

356
Sal.
- na-an. Ah! Ich ha-be ihn ge-küsst, dei-nen
- na-an. Ah! I have kissed thy
pp
p
Sal.
Mund, es war ein bit-te-rer Ge-schmack auf dei-nen Lip-pen
mouth, there was a bit-ter, bit-ter taste on thy red lips.
p
357
Sal.
Hat es nach Blut ge-schmeckt? Nein! Doch es schmeck-te viel-leicht nach
Was it the taste of blood? Nay! But per-chance this is the taste of
mf
espr.
pp
Sal.
Lie-be...
love...
molto espr.
mf
ppp
p

Sal.
Sie sa-gen, dass die Lie - be bit - ter schmecke...
They say that love hath a bit - ter taste...
mf
Al-lein was tut's?
But what of that?
molto espr.
mf
Was tut's?
What of that?
f
p
359
M. ♩: 60.
Ich ha-be deinen Mund ge -
I have now kissed thy
ff
360
küsst, Jo-cha - na - an. Ich ha-be ihn ge-küsst
mouth, Jo-ka - na - an. I have now kissed
dim.
molto espr.

A. 5503 F.

Sal.
ritard.
molto largo
sehr breit
361
(A moonbeam falls
(Der Mond bricht
dei - nen Mund.
thy mouth.
ff
sfz
on Salomé, covering her with light.)
wieder hervor und beleuchtet Salome.)
Herod (turning round)
Herodes (sich umwendend)
schneller
frei
Man tö - te dieses
Go, kill at once that
ritard.
più mosso
dim.
ff
Hero-des.
Molto allegro
Sehr schnell.
(Die Soldaten stürzen sich auf Salome und begraben sie unter ihren Schilden.)
362
Weib!
wench!
(The soldiers rush forward and crush Salomé under their shields.)
M. 𝅗𝅥=80.
(Curtain.)
(Der Vorhang fällt schnell.)

DATE DUE

Zeitfracht Medien GmbH
Ferdinand-Jühlke-Straße 7
99095 Erfurt, Deutschland
produktsicherheit@kolibri360.de